THE
HAND
OF
MID
NIGHT

THE
HAND
OF
MID
NIGHT

D.R. SELKIRK

atmosphere press

*This story is dedicated to Les Duntsch, my junior year
English teacher, who told me that I should be a writer
a long time ago.*

.

LOST AND FOUND

The day's sun was taking a peremptory bow on another late spring day. It was breaking into long thin shards of fading light that gradually disappeared into an even paler orb in the sky before one could not look at it anymore. The nights were steadily becoming warmer, and this heralded the ever-nearing arrival of the summer season; complete with groups of curious tourists who strayed off the beaten path to see what else they could find. They were usually looking for something a little more unusual and different from what the roadside tourist traps had to offer, finding instead a lovely little oasis seemingly in the middle of nowhere: Darmer Falls, Indiana. It was a small midwestern town named for one of the founding pioneer patriarchs of the last century: Francis J. Darmer. It had that quaint small-town charm. It was perfect. He could hardly wait...

Mike Rancic stretched out lazily and slowly on one of the benches in the park near his home. It was a park that was much larger than the small space that he currently occupied. At first glance, it appeared to be no more than a small gathering place for mothers with small children and assorted others. He stared off over the berm to his right, wondering as to all the mysteries that the twenty-five-acre landmass beyond had to offer. It was like a wild preserve that he hadn't had the chance to explore just yet, but maybe in a few weeks, when the weather turned a little warmer, he would do just that. Just to see what was on the other side of the boundaries of this small space, if nothing else.

He contemplated all these things to come as he sat relaxing in the sun, letting it sparsely warm him. That, and the latest case he was working on. Not for much longer, he thought. The sunlight would fade soon, and the spring air would turn cool. A little too cool for sitting around in a park, especially at night. As he looked around, people were already heading home for dinner or to other places where they needed to be. Mothers grabbed the hands of small children, and lovers ambled off together in one direction or another; just wanting to be with each other. Mike figured that he might as well rise to the occasion and get going too. He ran his fingers through his dark wavy hair that was beginning to show the first signs of gray as he rose from his comfortable spot on the far side park bench and followed the rest of the crowd in the general direction to the gate that everyone else had passed through on their way to wherever it was, they were headed next.

On his way out of the park, he saw a group of teenagers moving in his general direction. They all appeared to be dressed almost entirely in black, from head to toe. There were about five of them. They were talking, laughing, and snickering in a way that kids of that age were generally known to do. Damn kids, he thought. He had a fleeting memory of himself at that age, but to be fair his life had been a bit more serious at that point than the lives of these teens appeared to be at the moment. It made him think again about his latest case; a missing seventeen-year-old boy from a local family.

The boy, Jeremy Kinnon, had been missing for a little over a month and a half now, and Mike was beginning to feel a bit of frustration with the whole thing because he hadn't been able to turn over a single lead in all that time—which was unusual. He was used to having at least some idea of what was happening, or at least what had happened by this point in his investigation. He was three weeks in, and he had none. He needed to be able to tell this kid's parents something, and soon, and not what he thought was really going on, either. That their son was holed up somewhere with a bunch of his idiot friends, partying till all hours of the night, sleeping most of the day, and if he was lucky, having clumsy drunken romantic encounters somewhere in between. Still, that didn't explain why he hadn't been able to gain any leads on where the kid was at, or even where he had been since he disappeared. He needed to give this kid's parents closure of a sort, one way or another. He had wished for that ever since his own parents had died suddenly in an auto accident. Even though he had known what had happened to them, it always seemed like they were there one day and gone the next. Just there, and then they weren't. Forever. Almost like they had never really been. The memory was still painful for him even all these years later. It was like a dull ache in the center of his chest. It was never far out of reach and almost always close enough to touch. For this reason, Mike promised himself that he would hit the trail and hit it hard first thing tomorrow morning and come up with something, anything.

As he walked along lost in his own thoughts, the group of teenagers neared him. One in particular seemed to take keen notice of him. The others were too involved in their own conversations to care or look up. Mike couldn't hear what they were saying, just a bunch of indistinct secretive murmuring, and then he got the oddest sensation; like the hair standing up on the back of his neck. The last time he had had that sensation, he had found himself in the middle of a fire fight that he almost hadn't made it out of. No warning, nothing, not even an inkling of what was about to happen next, and in less time than it took for him to breathe or think about it, he was up to his neck in a situation that had almost cost him his life. He had gotten that same heebie jeebie feeling about two minutes before all hell had broken loose. He was getting that same feeling now to a slightly lesser degree. It said "Danger".

He looked up to see a boy from the group who looked to be about fifteen or sixteen years old with dirty blonde hair, wide eyes, and flaring nostrils regarding him intently. Almost too intently. The late afternoon sun had almost completely faded to dusk, and he couldn't be sure, but he thought he saw some kind of a red glow behind the kid's eyes just for the briefest second. He realized it had to be a trick of the light. There was no such thing as camera shadows in real life. It was a trick of film.

Just then he caught the barest hint of an old familiar scent he knew, but he couldn't quite place. It was too faint and too deeply buried in his memory. It added to that unsettled feeling he was getting. Mike decided at that point, that he was extremely tired and, in all likelihood, over-thinking the situation, not to mention the entire case and everything else connected with it. It was time for him to get home, grab some dinner, get some sleep, and start fresh tomorrow.

As the group neared him, they seemed to collectively veer off in another direction all together as if they were trying to avoid him completely. He looked at the pack with mild regard and smiled and waved. Another one of the teens looked at him. This one looked a little more familiar; almost like the kid he had been looking for, but he couldn't quite be sure in the dusky light of early evening. He looked to be about the right age, height, and build, but then they all looked pretty much the same at this age. The way they dressed, and talked, and shuffled along aimlessly going nowhere. The light was fading, and he was tired. He decided it was best to tackle it tomorrow. He continued on toward home without giving it much more thought than that.

The next day Mike pulled out his file on Jeremy Kinnon. The boy was nearly eighteen years old, a ne'er do well kid with low aspirations, a likely outcast, and probably bullied by the jocks at school—not to mention angry and depressed. He was familiar with the breed. He had seen a lot of them in the service. If they made it all the way through basic training, they usually got shipped out to foreign theaters of combat two months later. A good number of them never returned. If they did return, it wasn't too long until they were either locked up in jail or the loony bin. That, or heavily addicted to some narcotic. Either way, they had a harder time fitting into society when they came home than they had before they left. It was a sad statistic, but it was part of the circle of life as he knew it.

As for his story, after he had lost his parents suddenly to a car accident when he was twelve years old, he had gone to live with his mother's sister, Dona. She had been his only surviving blood relative that anyone could find. He felt like he had lost everything at that point. People had come around for almost two weeks, bringing food and flowers and prayers. He had cordially thanked them all but had kept his distance. At that moment, he erected an invisible wall around himself that he kept in place until the day he shipped out for basic training. Then he fortified it, as he was being shepherded into to his new life and shipped off to a foreign soil to fight against a people that he neither knew nor had any quarrel with that he was aware of.

Aunt Dona had given him an old Greek medal with the image of a titan with an angel on his shoulder as a protection from harm. She told him that his grandfather had carried that same medal through World War II and had come home safely. According to her, it had protected his grandfather from all things, and it would protect him too. As she hugged him and cried, she tearfully reassured him that he had been chosen for great things and that he would come through this. The fates would bring him back home safely. That had been almost twenty-five years ago. He had been trained as a medic, where he helped to treat and aid the dead and the dying. In his short tour of war, he had seen more death and dying than he cared to remember. After that, all he wanted to do was to come home and forget. Sometimes with the aid of a strong drink or two that he referred to as his "warming medicine."

When he returned home, he had decided to start a private investigation service. Although it managed adequately, he knew he would never wind up on the cover of Fortune 500. It paid the bills, and he could make his own hours. There was also the added benefit of not having a boss directing his every move at every given second of the day. Life was good enough for what it was for the time being.

Aunt Dona had passed last year. She sat down one day in the late afternoon sun and had dozed off and never woke up. An autopsy revealed that she had had an aneurysm that had burst as she sat there peacefully napping. She hadn't suffered; she was just gone. Just like his parents. Just as well, he thought, she was a good woman and deserved to leave this life peacefully. As far as he was concerned, she had done more than her part by taking him in and taking care of him all those years ago. She had raised him to be strong and to carry on no matter what, instilling in him a sense of duty that was still with him to this day. She didn't have to, but she had. He was grateful that she had been there for him when he had needed it most. Now she was at peace, and he hoped with his parents somewhere. It was at that moment, he realized how truly alone in the world he was. So be it, he thought. It had been that way since he was twelve. He said his goodbyes and God-speed to her in a silent prayer on a warm fall day while the warm wind blew the autumn leaves around in circles at his feet. He silently asked her to say hello to his parents when she saw them.

After that, he left quietly without alerting any of the other funeral guests and headed out on the road with everything he owned, which fit into a couple of duffle bags and a box thrown into the bed of his Toyota pickup the previous evening. He landed in Darmer Falls two weeks later. Three weeks after that he had opened Rancic Private Investigations and had drummed up enough business to survive through the winter and a bit beyond. Now it was spring, and he was thinking about maybe moving down the road again, but he needed to finish the cases he had open first. Namely, Jeremy Kinnon. If for no other reason than the kid's parents needed to know what had happened to their son, and they all needed closure. The challenge of finding out was also beginning to make him a little more than mildly curious and just a bit edgy.

It was another warm afternoon, back on the same little bench in the same little park pondering the same mysteries of life and disappearance. Mike was still no closer to the answer he was looking for than he had been the day before and the day before that. Again, the sun was again beginning to gently fade in order to make way for evening. He rose dutifully from his bench as he did on so many afternoons and made his way toward the park exit. All the other families and assorted others had already left. Alone as always, this it seemed was destined to be his lot in life.

Just then, he heard a twig snap behind him. Odd he thought, he could have sworn he was the only one left here. As he turned to confront the source of the sound, he came face to face with a teen who he was sure had been with the group he had seen yesterday. As he stared into the face of a boy who appeared to be about seventeen or eighteen years of age, he felt slightly chilled. If he didn't know better, he would swear this was the same kid he had been looking for the past three-and-a-half weeks. The difference was that this boy seemed to have a dangerous air about him that he couldn't quite put his finger on, but he could feel it. If this was indeed the same kid, he had changed a lot in three weeks. Either that, or the picture that Jeremy's parents had given Mike didn't do the kid justice at all.

"I hear you been looking for me," the kid said in a husky voice that was almost close to a snarl and seemed to conceal his age a bit, but not his apparent strength.

"Looking for you?" Mike asked in a careful tone. "Do I know you?" He followed up carefully, trying to size up the situation.

"Yeah, you know who I am," the boy replied without looking up as he walked around in a small circle, like a caged animal stalking restlessly, Mike thought. It was true. Mike had figured it out almost immediately. Although this kid still didn't look like the one in the picture except for the obvious resemblance, he could see enough other similarities that made him pretty sure that this was, in fact, the same kid he had been looking for. The boy had the same square jaw line as the kid in the picture. The same shoulders that were beginning to broaden, announcing to the world that he was leaving the physicality of a boy behind to step into the shoes of a man, but most of all, the piercing stare when he was looking right at you, but seemed to be looking elsewhere at the same time. It was the first thing Mike had noticed in the photograph that Jeremy's parents had given him to work with. This version however, had a few minor/major alterations. Those being that he looked slightly older than his stated age, but not by much. He walked with the power and grace of an apex predator; one that was trying to hide his obvious strengths, but not really succeeding. Also, other than appearing extremely pale, he gave the impression of a near perfect physical specimen. It was unsettling how a few minor differences painted an entirely different picture of someone, he thought.

Mike looked around to see if anyone else was still here besides the two of them. The park was empty. Then, without warning, the kid closed the distance between the two of them so quickly that Mike didn't even have time to react. He stepped back quickly, instinctually.

"Take it easy old man, I won't bite you," the kid said with an almost wicked smile on his lips. Mike wasn't sure why, but this kid was unnerving the hell out of him and didn't seem to really be trying all that hard.

"What about your parents?" Mike asked.

"What about them?" the kid shot back. "They're too busy with their own pathetic lives to even take notice of what's going on with me or the rest of the world."

"Don't you think they're worried about you and want to know where you've been?" Mike asked.

"Why should they be?" the kid asked. "I can take care of myself. Just like I did before this, when they were supposed to be looking out for me. Only I don't need them anymore," he said with a hint of bitterness in his voice.

"I know your mother is worried," Mike said. "She was the one who sent me to find you."

"Really?" the kid asked, as if he found that fact amusing. "It would have been nice if I had known she cared so much before."

"Before what?" Mike asked, trying to make the conversation flow.

"It doesn't matter," the kid responded in a hushed, almost reverent tone. "It's a done deal now."

"Well, you might want to give her a call," Mike said. "Just to let her know you're okay, if nothing else."

"I'll think about it," the kid replied.

Just then the breeze shifted ever so slightly, and Mike caught a whiff of the same scent that he'd had trouble placing the evening before. The one he couldn't quite recognize because it was too faint but still familiar and deeply buried in his memory. The odor was stronger now, and he recognized it immediately. It was blood; old blood to be exact. It was blood mixed with the scent of death. The kind of terrifying death that an animal experiences when it's caught in the jaws of a superior predator, knowing that there is no escaping its fate. Mike felt a sudden wave of nausea kick in. There was an uncontrollable instinctual animal terror welling up inside him. It started in the pit of his stomach, that seemed to hit bottom like a broken carnival ride pitching off the edge of the tracks as it rounded a turn. As his fear took on a life of its own, it crawled steadily up from his stomach and into his throat, then slid back down between his shoulder blades till it reached his lower back, leaving him feeling deathly ill. He could feel a chilled sweat begin to bead on the back of his scalp and neck and between his shoulder blades as he realized that the smell he recognized, had something to do with this kid and the fact that he seemed so unusually powerful and dangerous. He just didn't know what, not yet, but he would find out. Later. Right now, all his senses were telling him to get gone as fast as he could.

It was almost dark now and Mike all at once realized his folly in not leaving the park earlier when he should have. As he stood there making small talk with the kid, he was trying desperately to formulate a plan in the back of his mind, to get himself out of this situation with as few bumps, and bruises, or worse as possible. He didn't know why, but his gut instinct was telling him that something far beyond his surface level understanding was way off here. He also realized on an entirely instinctual level that this was a dance between predator and prey, and he didn't need to think on it too hard to figure out which role he was playing. Jeremy, for his part seemed slightly amused. Like a cat watching a mouse that it's considering devouring but hasn't quite made up its mind yet.

Finally, Jeremy spoke. "So, what's your name?" he asked almost teasingly; the wicked smile starting to light his mouth again.

"Mike, Mike Rancic," Mike replied shakily.

"Well, Mike Rancic, where do we go from here?"

"You tell me," Mike responded with more bravado than he actually felt. "As for myself, I need to get home to dinner and some other paperwork right now. Maybe we can talk about it in a couple of days?" Mike offered amicably. He had no intention of meeting up with this kid ever again if he could help it. He was done; out of here as they say. All he had to do was get out of this park in one piece tonight, and it was over for him. He would tell Jeremy Kinnon's parents that he had been unable to find their son or any information about what had happened to him. He would take a bow and then he would make plans to leave town the next week. He was pretty sure that they wouldn't be too excited to meet Jeremy 2.0 that he had found tonight. At the very least, he figured he would be doing them a favor.

Mike shivered inwardly once more as a picture flashed through his mind again of a gazelle caught in the jaws of a lion as its life ebbed away. He jammed his hand into his right pocket, fiddling with some bits of lint and spare change, searching intently for the medal Aunt Dona had given him. His hand finally closed around it, giving him a sense of comfort and courage. He had carried it with him always, ever since he had been in the service. It had carried him through many dark places and brought him out on the other side; just like Aunt Dona had said it would. At that moment, Jeremy turned to look at Mike with such an intense stare that Mike felt as if Jeremy could read his thoughts. That uneasy feeling of the evening before began to plague him in earnest once again. As he looked into Jeremy's eyes, he could see the animal. Jeremy didn't look human anymore. It was terrifying on its own level.

"Trust me, it won't help you as much as you hope it can," Jeremy held out in an almost mocking tone. "Faith and deter-mination are the only things that will see you through in the end, and even those will fail you half of the time," he finished without bitterness or regret—only acceptance.

"I'll keep that in mind," Mike said evenly, trying to control his fear and keep his voice from shaking.

"Well, it's time for me to go," Jeremy said flatly. "I have other business to attend to as well. What was that you mentioned earlier? Dinner? Ah yes, dinner. I could do with a bit of that myself. It's okay, we'll talk again soon. Till then, take care Mike Rancic."

"You too," Mike responded a lot more casually than he felt as he headed in the direction of the gate. He couldn't get there fast enough in his mind. As he was walking away, he looked up and saw the same group of teens that Jeremy had been with the day before. They were walking on the small berm hillside just on the other side of the park, headed for the wilderness area. They had a more hardened look now, predatory like Jeremy, only worse. Jeremy crossed to the other side of the park to meet up with them and climbed the small hill where they were standing, with seemingly no effort at all and in record time. As the group took off together, Mike could hear them talking and laughing in low hushed tones and... snickering... wickedly... Mike felt just like a cat that had just used up at least two to three of his nine lives or more in one shot.

When he reached home, Mike locked the door and turned on every light in the house. After that, he reached into the cabinet containing his warming medicine as he liked to call it— a bottle of hundred proof bourbon and a set of glasses. He took out the bottle and a glass. After taking a couple of swallows directly from the bottle, he poured some of the amber liquid into a glass. He was shaking so violently that he could barely hold it steady enough to bring it to his lips without sloshing it all over the place. He was still shaking after two more shots. He knew that what he had come in contact with tonight had no rational explanation, and he was afraid to let his mind give him the answer he knew was there. It was the stuff of ghost stories and legends. It wasn't real. There was no way it could be he thought. Still, his mind had no rational explanation for what he had experienced tonight, only the way it had made him feel. He felt more afraid than he could ever remember feeling in his entire life. Even when he had been in the middle of battle. What his gut instinct was screaming at him, his rational mind would not let him accept. Not yet. He tossed down a couple more shots, and before he knew it, he had put a pretty good dent in the bottle's contents and had dozed off into a fitful sleep.

When Mike woke up the next morning, there was a patch of sunlight painted on the carpet in the middle of his room. The room was bright and peaceful and seemingly normal. This included the clothes strewn about on the floor and over a single chair from the last couple days. His head hurt and his stomach had that scoured out feeling from too much drink the night before. He really needed to stop reaching for the warming medicine so much he thought. He started thinking back on the events of the previous evening and eventually he decided it must have been a bad dream. Then, just for the heck of it, he grabbed the pair of jeans he had been wearing the night before and jammed his hand into the right front pocket, searching for the medal. It wasn't there. His heart seemed to skip a beat as he held his breath almost simultaneously. It was always there. Right in the right front pocket of whatever pair of pants he happened to be wearing at the time, nestled between all the spare change, funny bits of lint, and an odd assortment of keys that he usually carried. It wasn't there. He took a deep, full breath, realizing that he must have dropped it somewhere, possibly in the house or at the park the night before. He suddenly realized at almost the same moment that if he remembered being at the park last night, then everything else must also be real. He shuddered at the thought that this could even be a possibility.

He began searching every place in the house he could think of where the medal might have dropped, or that he might have placed it. Under furniture, in drawers, even in the washing machine and dryer. No dice. The medal wasn't anywhere to be found. He knew where he had to look next. He made his way back to the park. Everything there looked calm and serene and completely normal. It was sunny and beautiful. All the mothers with small children, and lovers who just wanted to be with each other had returned. There was nothing odd or out of place like the night before. He searched all along the ground and through the various tufts of multi-colored grass, as well as at the bases of the different trees there. All to no avail. The medal was nowhere to be found. Mike finally gave up after about three hours. This was something he was not accustomed to doing. He couldn't believe that he had lost the talisman that had carried him through some of the darkest times of his life for so many years. As he was trying to decide what his next move would be, he decided to pay a visit to Jeremy Kinnon's parents.

As he walked through the middle-class neighborhood on the edge of suburban blight that had once been the toast of the town, he studied the signs of aging and neglect. Peeling paint, curling roof shingles, and dry brown grass. He finally stopped at an older home where the gate needed to be mended and painted, and the fence and porch looked like it could do with some attention as well. He knocked on a dilapidated screen door that appeared to be the original door that had been built with the house. A small pale woman cautiously answered the door, pulling it open just a crack and peeking out through it. It was Jeremy's mother, Claire. Mike asked her if he could come inside and discuss the case for a bit. She obliged, almost unwillingly. As he stepped into the house across the threshold, he could see even in the hazy dim light of late afternoon that the woman in front of him looked sick. More like scared sick. It was the kind of sick that make-up and clothes and even bravado can't hide. She looked like someone frightened out of her wits to the core. It was like she had seen something her eyes couldn't believe, and her mind couldn't accept. Mike knew just what that felt like. As he looked around the house, the tightly drawn shades and a dimly lit interior reminded him more of a bunker than a house. She offered him coffee, which he politely declined.

"Claire," he said her name gently. "I have been working Jeremy's case for a little over three weeks now, trying to find out exactly what happened to your son. As much as it pains me to admit it, I'm fresh out of leads." The woman in front of him looked as if she were about to cry, and then stoically straightened her posture in acceptance of the situation. They talked for a while about the night that Jeremy disappeared. The fight with his father and all the things that had led up to it that had finally ended with Jeremy leaving. That was the last time they had seen him.

Mike asked her where Jeremy's father was. Claire told him he was still at work. The truth was that he had been on a bender for the last two days. Claire was content to let him stay gone because when he came home after one of those, life was not happy in the Kinnon household. Not for a while, until her husband got fully sober. He would then cry and promise not to drink or smack anyone around anymore because of his stress with the job, the kid, the mortgage, and anything else that he could tack on to that to excuse his abominable behavior. She had always hoped that one day he would just stay gone. She gave Mike a weak smile and thanked him for all he had done, as she showed him to the door. Mike told her he would let her know if anything else turned up, but for the moment, things were pretty much at a standstill. He wasn't okay with charging an already financially constrained couple more money for no results he thought. With that, he said his goodbyes and left.

As he began walking back home along the same route he had come, there was an almost frigid breeze blowing down the street in the late afternoon sun. Evening was already beginning to make its presence felt and there was a definite chill in the air. Mike hadn't meant to stay so long with Jeremy's mother, but he had had the feeling that she needed a bit of human understanding that she hadn't been able to find in quite some time. That, and they had talked about everything that had led up to Jeremy's disappearance in a lot more detail than they had previously. They talked about Jeremy's relationship with his father, all culminating in the fight that had ended with him storming out of the house about a month and a half ago. His parents thought he'd be back after a couple of nights when he cooled off, but that hadn't happened. A week and a half later they rang Mike to see if he could find out where their son had gotten off to. Three weeks later Mike was still at square one.

As he walked past the little park that he so often sat in during the day to do his thinking work, he thought he'd have one last look around really quick to see if he could spot the medal on the ground anywhere. As he was visually skimming the ground and getting ready to give up, he heard a crackle behind him and turned around. He knew even before he turned around that it was Jeremy. He was alone.

"Looking for this?" Jeremy asked as he held up the well-worn medal. "I found it here on the ground after you left last night. You must have dropped it," he said, the wicked smile lighting his mouth again. Mike felt the familiar welling of fear inside him again, although not as starkly as the evening before. He was almost beginning to get used to the idea of this edge of danger scenario he thought.

"Yes," Mike said. "Thank you for finding it," he replied with focused calm.

"Here," Jeremy tossed the medal almost carelessly to Mike. Mike caught it with a little more effort extended than he would have liked. It felt good as he closed his hand around it once again; almost like a piece of himself had been returned to him. Jeremy seemed to be studying him and then, as Mike looked up, Jeremy's face shifted into neutral all at once, but his eyes never did.

"Well, I just wanted to get that back to you," Jeremy said. "Remember what I told you before," he added. Then he was off. Walking away, or more aptly floating, with almost no sound at all, like a predator getting ready to hunt. Mike didn't need a billboard sign to let him know that he was free to go. As soon as Jeremy was far enough away, he moved toward the gate as quickly as he could without running.

Mike reached his little bungalow on the east side of town in what seemed to him like record time. As he stepped through the door, he noticed the lights were on. Dimly lit, but nevertheless on. Funny, he didn't think that he'd left them on... as he was pondering this fact and looking around to reset his boundaries, he heard a voice that was startlingly deep and masculine and clearly dangerous.

"Good evening," the dark stranger said in greeting. He was sitting on the couch in Mike's living room with his legs crossed comfortably and his arms spread across the back of it as if he were lounging in a club den or an old friend's house.

"My name is Pathos," the stranger drooled the words out carefully so that Mike wouldn't miss anything in the translation. Mike took in the impeccably tailored black clothing, the ultra-smooth skin, the far too pale complexion, and of course the almost imperceptible red glow behind the eyes. It was another one of them. "I'm here about a mutual friend of ours, Jeremy Kinnon? I believe you've recently made his acquaintance." The stranger flashed a slightly twisted smile as he said this, letting his words hang in the air for maximum effect.

There was an invisible evil essence that crept forth from him with every word he spoke.

"Maybe," Mike said as studied the stranger a little more carefully. "Can I ask why that gives you the right to barge into my home uninvited?" he asked as he attempted to keep his voice from shaking. Pathos made an odd clicking noise with his mouth as a wicked grin began to spread across his face.

"Oh dear, you really shouldn't believe everything you read in stories. Everyone knows that" he said almost mockingly. "I'll come straight to the point. Our little friend Jeremy and some of his cohorts are playing a very unwise game. You see, Jeremy is my newest, how should I say it? Employee? Minion? Thrall? To put it directly, young Jeremy should be about my business, and not his own."

"And that has what to do with me, exactly?" Mike asked evenly.

"Well, you are in the business of finding people, are you not? I could certainly do it myself, but I have other more pressing matters to attend to at the moment. So, when you see our young friend next, please convey to him it would be in his best interest to come and find me before I find him. Oh yes, and there would be the matter of your fee," he said, and with that he pulled a stack of tightly bundled money from his coat pocket that was as impeccably gathered as his clothing and laid it on the coffee table. "Please, don't disappoint me," he said as he looked away, "I tend not to deal with disappointment very well," he drawled out in an almost absentminded tone, but Mike caught the cruel glint in his eyes as a twisted smile tried to curve around his too thin harsh line of a mouth. Mike certainly didn't need a translator to tell him that as scary as he thought Jeremy was, this guy was at least five hundred notches farther up the food chain and at least that much more dangerous. The kid was in way over his head and Mike had found more trouble than he realized. He also didn't need a translator to tell him that like it or not, he was now a part of this drama. He couldn't help thinking that he should have left well enough alone when he'd had the chance. Now he was swimming in the same drowning pool with Jeremy.

"I'll do that," Mike said as he turned his back on the interloper to reach into the cupboard for his warming medicine. He pulled down the bottle and two glasses with the expectation of offering his guest a drink. As he turned around to make the offer, he realized that the stranger who had so brazenly invaded his home was gone. Everything was silent, normal looking. Had he imagined everything? The conversation that had just taken place? No, it was real, alright. The money the stranger had left was still sitting quietly on the table. His reeling mind was now beginning to accept what his core had been trying to tell him all along. This was real. In that moment of abject clarity, he suddenly understood that ignorance really was bliss—more often than not. The next step he thought, was to track down Jeremy and get some answers as to the rest of what this was really all about. It was a relief, he thought, when you finally accept the truth of a situation and no longer feel the need to pretend. You're freer than you ever imagined. Hence, that old saying that "the truth will set you free". He felt almost relieved at his core. Now he needed to focus on the business of survival, if that were even still on the table at this point.

He decided to head back to the park once again. He felt like some weirdo predator after dark. If they only knew the half of it, he thought and smiled derisively to himself as he sat there in the dark, waiting. Finally, he heard the familiar snap of twigs and leaves and other debris as Jeremy seemed to just be there suddenly, as if he had come from nowhere.

"Mike," he said in that all too familiar voice. "I didn't know you were the kind to sit around in a park after dark," pleased with his own humor.

"I'm not," Mike retorted. "Except when I'm looking for a local missing kid that's not really missing."

"Oh, that."

"Yeah, that." Mike did his best to let his sarcasm show through. It made him feel as though there was at least a partial element to the situation that he was able to control. "I had a visit of sorts from a friend of yours earlier tonight."

"Pathos" Jeremy said flatly, already knowing the answer without having to ask the question. Mike's fear was giving way just enough to let his curiosity peek through. He began to understand with sudden clarity that Jeremy was trying to do the same thing that he was. Survive.

Mike gave Jeremy a nod and the general gist of the visit, along with Pathos' dire warning.

"So, what now?" Mike asked as he stared bleakly off into space. Jeremy knew at this point, he had to come clean and divulge all of the ugly secrets that he'd been living for almost the past two months or so. This was not going to be easy as he was just beginning to come to terms with it himself. In fact, it was the hardest thing that he could ever remember having to do besides leaving his parents' house that night. How could he possibly begin to explain the truth of the situation he had been living with and through? he silently wondered to himself. No time like the present, he thought, here goes.

"I suppose you've connected the dots and figured it out by now." Jeremy let his obvious secret escape his lips with a brief exhalation as he felt himself struggling to take his next breath.

"Yeah," Mike said quickly. "You're not supposed to exist. You're the stuff of legend and campfire stories."

"If only it was really that simple," Jeremy responded almost bleakly.

"So, what now?" Mike asked as Jeremy took a seat beside him on the ground in the chilled night air and said,

"Now we must make ready to fight. Make no mistake my

friend, there's a battle on its way here whether we prepare or not, but there are some things I need to tell you about first," and with that, Jeremy began to recount the story of the night his whole life was forever changed. The night he became more than just another sad kid out for some laughs and a good time with his friends, trying to escape the dysfunction of his parents' home. All those events seemed to have a dreamlike quality to them now; so surreal.

He had stormed out of his parents' home that night, vowing never to come back, and going nowhere in particular. He had run into Pathos as he sat waiting at a bus stop. The two had struck up a conversation. This stranger was charismatic and filled him with impossible stories of wonder far beyond anything that he could really imagine or had experienced in his short life to that point. These stories held possibilities that he wanted so badly to believe in. Pathos had told him how he could be something so much more than he was at that moment; a force to be reckoned with, having the ability to experience things at a level far beyond what he could imagine now. He would be the envy of all who met him. It sounded almost too good to be true, like everything he had ever dreamt about or wanted, but was not sure how to reach. Then Pathos offered him a strong drink from the flask he carried....

Jeremy woke up the next day in what appeared to be an old, abandoned building on the edge of town. He didn't recognize it. He also couldn't remember much of what had happened. He vaguely remembered meeting and talking to Pathos the night before. He felt weak and sore and sick all over. His right shoulder hurt like it was on fire. He twisted painfully as best he could to get a look at the source of the pain. It looked like he had sustained some kind of wound that he couldn't remember getting. It was beginning to crust over with dried blood. All he knew was that he felt sicker than he had ever been in his life and that he was having trouble moving. The light seemed to hurt his eyes and his skin, and it was making everything thing worse somehow. He let himself slip back into a fitful sleep of sorts.

A few hours later Jaxon showed up at dusk. Jaxon, who Jeremy didn't know at the time but who would later become his closest ally in this situation. Jaxon helped him, taking him to a large dark house a few miles away. A safe place he had called it. It was a large house out in the country on the edge of town, behind a large wrought-iron gate. Jeremy remembered being lost in a dreamlike state as he dreamt of fire, laughter, and blood—especially blood. He had nightmares and then they fled. He was fed a warm, thick life-giving liquid that calmed the pain inside him and the nightmares. After several days he came to.

As he struggled to focus and take in his surroundings, he began to feel his flesh tingling as it came suddenly alive. So alive it seemed to almost to take on a life of its own. He mused as he remembered how he began to grow stronger; feeling what seemed like a superhuman strength. That strength made him feel like he could almost tear apart buildings with his bare hands. His senses were also incredibly heightened and ultra-fine-tuned even without focus. He could hear and smell things at a distance, and he could move with incredible speed and agility that astounded him.

At first, he thought he must be imagining all of this, or having some kind of strange lucid waking dream. It was like being inside one of the video games he used to play. Then, after a while, he came to realize that it was actually happening. He wondered oddly if it had something to do with his wound. This was because all these abilities seemed to present themselves right after his injury. He also noticed that he seemed to have a fondness for the night too, cool breezes and freedom. The night sounds were like music to his ears. This was of course before he came to the realization of exactly who and what he was now.

THE HUNT

Approximately a week after Jaxon had brought him to the house, Jeremy woke not knowing what day or time it was. It must be almost evening he thought. He rose and stretched walking over to the mirror in his room. He was surprised to see how pale he had become. He stretched his left hand up to his face and then to his right shoulder blade, tugging back his shirt to reveal the wound on his shoulder. He wanted to see if it had healed. It had, but in its place an odd scar had been left. It resembled a birthmark that looked sort of like a dagger with a three-loop handle. He decided to ask about it later. He walked over to the heavy black curtains in his room, which were tightly drawn across the window. He wanted to get a peek at the outside world once again now that he was feeling better. He pulled back the curtain ever so slightly and a weak ray of sunshine touched his right forearm, which began to smolder and burn. It was not yet quite dusk. He yelped quickly, pulling the curtain shut as the smell of his own flesh burning reached his nose. Jaxon was there instantly and noticed the burn on Jeremy's arm, which was already beginning to heal.

"What's happening to me?" Jeremy asked in a voice that was rife with heightened alarm.

"You are changing, and the change is almost complete." Jaxon replied in a calming tone.

"Changing how? Why does my skin react to the sun? Why does it make me feel sick, make my skin hurt?"

"Because you are not as you were. You are different now. You are a butterfly who used to be a caterpillar," Jaxon replied calmly with an intonation that suggested Jeremy shouldn't ask any more questions at the present time.

Just then a drink was brought to his room. The nourishment drink. He was not sure what it was exactly. It tasted almost metallic and kind of coppery, but he noticed that he always felt much better after he drank it. It had a taste that reminded him of the bloody noses he used to get as a kid. The first smell of it would almost repulse him, but then within seconds his ravenous hunger, which seemed to completely envelop him, would take over and he would drink it down rapidly without another thought. Afterward, it was almost as if he would magically come to life with all his senses on high alert. It was like flipping on the switches that turn on a machine and bring it to life. Those first few minutes after nourishment were nothing short of amazing. He also started to notice that he didn't really remember eating any solid food lately but that he didn't seem to really miss it either. Although, because his mind had happened upon that thought, he asked Jaxon if they could go out and grab a burger.

"Soon," Jaxon had replied.

Two evenings later, Jaxon came to his room and said, "I have a surprise for you. We're going out on a hunt."

"A hunt?" Jeremy asked. "For what? Girls? Laughs? Money? What?"

"For food. The kind you can't get at the supermarket." Jaxon replied. Ten minutes later they were walking in a wooded area on the outskirts of town. Jeremy felt an almost childlike delight as the cool breeze filled his nostrils and the night sounds reached his ears. He couldn't explain exactly why, but he felt at one with the night, and it gave him a feeling of exhilaration all the same. Suddenly Jeremy heard the snapping of a twig and the rustling of leaves. He glanced in the direction of the sound. It was a yearling doe. She was foraging and suddenly halted her routine, standing absolutely stock still in an effort to hide in plain sight. Her nostrils flared ever so slightly. Silence. Jeremy could hear the elevated beating of her heart, and the silent labored breathing urged on by fear. There was also her imperceptible trembling as she attempted to avoid detection. Jeremy suddenly became aware of his own growing hunger and its almost overwhelming call. Suddenly there was a loud crack from a branch above as Jaxon descended rapidly down upon the doe, like an Angel of Death, breaking her spine. He began to feed on her blood, drinking from her jugular vein as if it were an open tap. She had attempted to flee just before, but her speed and timing were seconds too slow. It was clear that she was no match for the one who held her in his grasp now.

Jeremy looked into the doe's eyes as Jaxon continued to feed. He noted the look of fear and acceptance as her life force gradually left them. Jaxon looked up at Jeremy and offered to let him feed with him.

Something from deep inside him suddenly willed to cry out. It was the vague memory of the child that no longer existed; the human element of his being almost from before he was born. Jeremy stood there stunned, almost as still as the doe had been moments before. He could see an apparition of himself as a child, ethereal, as it floated in front of him. It reached out a hand to him with a strangled cry. As he reached back to grasp the hand that the apparition held out to him, the figure faded and disappeared. A single anguished tear stung Jeremy's eyes in a split second of mourning as he let go of the human innocence of his being. For a brief second, he considered refusing Jaxon's offer of food, but his hunger was so great that he was unable to control it as it directed him to feed. As he began to feed, the image of the child inside him faded from his consciousness, the way it had from his vision.

It continued to fade until it was gone. After a time, his rampant hunger was by no means sated. but was at least, temporarily held at bay.

As they walked home Jeremy asked Jaxon about the thing that they had done. Jaxon merely shrugged and replied,

"It's like I said. You're different now." Jeremy remembered the warm nourishment drink that he had been taking daily for the last week and a half. It tasted similar to the doe's blood, but slightly different. He asked Jaxon about this. Jaxon told him that to live is to feed and vice versa. The blood is the life, literally. Jaxon was clearly more accepting of these things than Jeremy was, which Jeremy accounted to time and knowledge. He asked Jaxon why they couldn't just rob a blood bank or something. Jaxon told him it was far too risky because of the possibility of being exposed to other people who would not understand, and secondly, there was no life force left in that blood. It dissipates as soon as the blood stops being pumped by a living heart. Further still, blood from one that has died will poison you, like a still stream. Death begets death. He told Jeremy that real nourishment comes from living blood. At that moment the realization of what he was now left him both stunned and terrified. He was so afraid to accept the idea that he could not even let his mind consider it at first.

"Don't worry, my friend Jaxon broke into his thoughts. You'll adapt. It's either that or you'll slowly fade and die. You must feed to live. Never forget that."

"I won't," Jeremy said almost absentmindedly, trying to mentally process the gravity of his situation as it was now.

Two nights later they went out again. This time closer to the township. There was a bar on the edge of town where a rougher crowd was known to hang out. Jaxon and Jeremy watched hidden in the shadows as people stumbled in and out; barely taking notice of what was around them. Jeremy felt unsure about this hunt. He wasn't sure that he could take a human life the way he had drained the doe of the last of hers. He felt nervous and fidgety as Jaxon focused intently on the comings and goings of the bar. After a momentary lull, a couple stumbled out of the open doorway toward the parking lot. Suddenly the woman pulled away from her partner and raised her voice in a heated tone. It was clear that the two were having some sort of disagreement. The man yelled at the woman and grabbed her arm roughly, telling her she better learn how to behave properly and mind her manners; like a lady if she knew what was good for her. She yelled louder and began to cry out as the man's grip tightened on her arm. Jaxon sprang into action, intercepting the couple in the middle of their discord.

"Hello," Jaxon said amicably to the couple. "I'm having a bit of car trouble and I need a hand to get her started. Could you possibly help me, sir?"

"Kid," the man slurred back, "can't you see that I'm in the middle of a conversation with the lady here?"

"I'm sorry, sir," Jaxon said almost a bit too contritely, looking down at the ground in mock desperation, "but I could really use your help getting her started, and then I'll be on my way."

"Okay, okay," the man sighed, leaving the smell of eighty proof hanging in the air. He turned back to his female companion and said, "You stay right here Myra, I'll be right back," and with that he followed Jaxon into the shadows, who promptly turned on him with bared teeth and glaring eyes filled with an unmistakable hunger; striking so rapidly that only a strangled squeal of air escaped the man's lips and nothing more. Jaxon drank deeply, sating his hunger and then dragged the body deeper into the woods for Jeremy to feed. Jeremy drank deeply as well, feeling his ever-present hunger begin to subside, but as his hunger faded, guilt took its place.

He was a killer now. It was something he had never

intended to be. Sure, he wanted to be stronger, faster, and better than he was; everybody wanted that, but not like this. This was dark and terrifying and most of all seemingly irreversible. As he fed, he thought about this. He thought about high school, with the cool kids sometimes making fun of him; about never quite measuring up or fitting in; and most of all about the girls who didn't even know that he existed. He wished, however briefly, that he could give them a preview of who he was now, so that he could relish and bask in the surprised and terrified looks on their faces. It would bring him such an incredible sense of satisfaction, but truthfully the only thing that he could think of at the moment was surviving. Living another day, both physically and with what he was.

This was where he ended the story as Mike attempted not to look as stricken as he felt. He actually felt kind of sorry for the kid, but just the smallest bit of fear kept getting in the way of that. He was not sure if that would pass with time, but right now there were bigger things to worry about; like how to contain Pathos. Pathos who had ceased to be anything that resembled something that had once been human a long time ago. The thought of even trying, made Mike shudder inwardly. Jeremy told Mike that they needed to meet again tomorrow night, here. He also told Mike that he was bringing friends; his kind, and he cautioned Mike to try to keep his fear at bay. Fear, he told Mike, was like catnip to a vampire, and was almost as irresistible as the blood itself.

"Don't worry, I'll be your protector," and with that he was off, vanishing as if he'd become part of the night.

Mike headed homeward in the dark, alone and unafraid, because he knew had already been face to face with the most dangerous thing out there – almost. As he entered his bungalow he smelled a strange odor, like something old and moldy, almost putrefying beneath the surface, but it was faint. As he racked his brain for what it might be and where it might be coming from, something grabbed him—hard. He felt the blackness closing in on him and his last recollection before everything went dark were a pair of glowing eyes and a cruel smile. When he finally came to, he was lying on the couch in his dimly lit living room trying to get his bearings and wondering what had happened. His head and neck felt as if he had been grabbed by Andre the Giant. As he struggled to focus, a familiar shape came into view. Pathos was sitting in an armchair directly across from him looking pathetically bored and slightly annoyed. He sat up abruptly.

"What are you doing in my house?" he asked, fighting to keep the note of fear out of his voice.

"Have you delivered my message to our young friend?" Pathos asked in that voice that told Mike that he not only knew the answer, but that he was toying with him.

"Yes," Mike answered.

"Good, I'll expect him within two days' time from now; and if he doesn't keep that appointment I will be forced to go and find him, and that my friend will be unfortunate for all concerned."

The meaning of Pathos' words was not lost on Mike. He sat there hoping that whatever the plan was to deal with this vampire psychopath, had a snowball's chance in hell of working. If not, he feared greatly for the aftermath. When he looked up, Pathos had vanished. Of course, he thought, survive the horrors of war and die at the hands of a bunch of frigging vampires. Totally normal.

STRATEGIES

The next evening, Mike made his way to the park with which he was becoming intimately familiar. He could identify one tree and bush from another almost right down to the tufts of grass on the ground. He knew where the all the rocks and the potholes were too, and even which birds frequented this particular park. Perfect, he thought sarcastically. At least I'm familiar with the terrain. Every good (or bad) battle plan starts there. He found his bench and decided to wait for Jeremy and his friends. His anxiety mounted as he waited. After a while he thought that they might have called it off and he was ready to leave and try again tomorrow. When he finally reached the point where he was getting ready to pack it in, he heard the familiar crackling of twigs and branches being broken under foot. He intuitively realized that this was for his benefit and his alone, as he knew that Jeremy and probably his friends as well could appear out of nowhere without making a sound. They were just there if they wanted to be.

Jeremy was first to materialize, and Mike realized that he was secretly grateful for this. It was a lot easier to pretend not to be afraid if you knew you had back up to begin with, regardless of how fleeting that might be. The next to show up were a pair of identical twin youths named Sercan and Saro (pronounced Sorrow). They looked as though had been teleported directly from Conan the Barbarian's time. They wore long black cloaks which barely concealed the swords and other crude but effective weaponry they wore. They were descended from generations of fearless Viking warriors. They stood next to each other stock still at attention as if waiting for the next order to be given. The two had shared a womb before their mortal lives had begun and had been inseparable ever since, even in death. They were literally brothers in arms, both in this life and the one that had preceded it, and they would be linked together in whatever life or lack of it they found themselves in next. One would never be without the other, ever. This was their bond.

Next came two extremely beautiful girls, both as different as night and day. This last thought Mike found amusing despite the obvious situation, because what was happening now would never and could never happen during daylight hours. The first girl had almost moonglow pale skin and a shimmering curtain of fire red hair. Her eyes were a striking green gold that resembled a cat's. They were like two mesmerizing hypnotic pools that one could drown in. The smell of her was like the slightest perfume of early evening as it followed her. The girl's name was Aconia.

The second girl also appeared as if from nowhere, dressed in a rich royal blue velvet cloak that surrounded her. Her skin was the color of a rich, dark exotic wood with long wavy ebony tresses that flowed down her back. She was slightly shorter in stature than Aconia, but her eyes reflected those of a strategist and battle-hardened warrior. It was clear to Mike that she had seen her share of battles both with a sword and without one. This he knew how to recognize from his own experience. This was the girl they called Onyx. She was also known as the Queen of midnight. Lastly, there was Jaxon who needed no introduction. He was Jeremy's best friend, partner, protector, and advisor of the moment. Jeremy squatted down next to Mike and asked, "Ready for this?"

"About as ready as I'll ever be," Mike replied. Aconia

immediately fixed her gaze on Mike; sniffing the air, a look of hunger beginning to show in her eyes. "I smell dinner..." she said with just a hint of malice in her voice.

"Not this one" Jeremy replied and met her gaze evenly.

"Do you forget that I can easily overpower you, new one? I am older than you," she declared in a mocking and petulant tone that she was clearly enjoying.

"No, I have not forgotten, Aconia, but have you forgotten that if you do, I will fight you no holds barred, and whichever of us takes the life of the other will be rendered into the hands of the Keeper? You are older than me, but I am quicker than you; strategically speaking. Ergo, nobody truly wins."

Aconia seemed to consider this fact briefly and let the matter drop for the moment. Experience had taught her that there would always be time to settle accounts later. Onyx watched quietly from a corner. Her acute skills of assessment were working the entire time. The twins remained as they had been from the beginning, stock still and soundless. This was not their argument.

Mike made no comment but was nonetheless impressed not to mention grateful by how well and quickly Jeremy had taken control of the situation and protected him in the process. He could see that Jeremy was clearly in the early stages of becoming much more than he was now at this very moment. Although this situation was far from what he would have chosen to be included in, Mike was nonetheless impressed with Jeremy's obvious progression. He felt as if he was looking at a future untested general. The boy was certainly progressing into far more than he had been a few weeks earlier.

Jeremy led the gathering, keeping all present focused on himself. "Pathos," he said, "has a very dangerous if not cataclysmic plan, as I have recently made all of you aware. I know this to be a fact because Jaxon and I were made aware when we were inducted and pulled in as his immediate thralls."

Jeremy let the weight of his words sink in before he continued. The fact that the rest of them had not yet been pressed into service toward the workings of this mad plan was a minor saving grace that he wanted them all to savor before he finished telling them about the potential destruction of life as they had come to know it.

The fact that he had known this life for only a short time was immaterial. There was a lot more at stake here than just the vampire world. There were two worlds about to collide and neither would survive that event to his limited reckoning if there were not an intervention of some kind. Pathos believed that he would rule whichever world survived, but Jeremy believed that there would be no survival for any if someone did not attempt to intervene. This is what had brought them here to this place. He wanted to live at least a little while longer. Even if it was in this world to which he had been born only a few short weeks ago. He was reasonably sure that he wasn't the only one, which was evidenced by his comrades in arms.

Jeremy began to address the group, choosing his words carefully, lest he lose the first battle before the war had begun.

"In the short time that I have been a part of this world, I have learned much more than I ever imagined was real or possible. When I lived in the human world, learning about our kind was an entertaining pastime of legends and stories and folklore. When I became a part of this world, I realized that there was so much more, and that learning was not only a pastime but a very necessary matter of survival, hence our meeting tonight." The others murmured their assent.

"So, what has dear old Pathos cooked up this time?" Aconia asked in a bitter tone. She had a particular distaste for the old but extremely powerful vampire. Ever since he had attempted to bind and enslave her as his mate a couple of centuries earlier. Fortunately for her, a house servant had taken pity on her and set her free, urging her to run. Run she had, but Pathos had recaptured her almost immediately. The house servant in question, though, had run as well and made his way to Dmitri, the most powerful vampire and leader of their kind at the present time. Dmitri had intervened on her behalf just in time. He had directed Pathos not only to set her free, but to leave her unharmed and unmolested.

Pathos, even for all his cunning, strength, and power did not dare to disobey or attempt to offer challenge, for to do so would have rendered him into the hands of the Keeper of the Second Night. The sleep from which one does not wake. That is, if he were to survive Dmitri's wrath beforehand.

Pathos grudgingly did as he was ordered, but Aconia always had the feeling that if the opportunity ever presented itself, he would one day attempt to even the score. For his part, he would have to elicit his revenge extremely carefully for Dmitri was not known to be merciful with those who betrayed or disobeyed him. Jeremy continued to explain to the group how Pathos had planned to build an army of new ones in order to usurp the power that he felt had been denied him for far too long. Pathos wanted to create a new world order. Jeremy also explained that to build this army many more ravins would need to be born into their world in record time. New ones, or ravins as they were sometimes called, are born ravenously hungry. They are extremely strong and twice as unpredictable, preying on anyone or anything within their reach. To feed is their only thought for some time.

Thus, when a ravin is born, they must be mentored and taught to control their urges. They must also learn to master their heightened senses. This is necessary in order to help them protect their extreme vulnerabilities. Without this time of mentoring, they become heightened killing machines without direction. This process of learning and understanding is somewhat lengthy. Jeremy had not been afforded the time of learning that a ravin should have. Luckily in his case, he

adapted so naturally and quickly that even Jaxon was surprised. Jaxon would not have been as surprised if he had
known that Jeremy had always been able to learn things at an
incredibly accelerated rate, faster than most when he was
human. He had just never applied his talents where anyone
could take notice of them. That, and becoming a vampire had
enhanced these qualities dramatically. It was like he was
somehow always meant for this life. This was a fortunate
circumstance, as in the present situation, time was of the
essence. This, however, was not the norm in their world. To
produce so many ravins in such a short time would fatalis-
tically alter the balance that had allowed their kind to survive
for so long. Their world lived in shadows; written off as a
fantasy of lore. For humans to become undeniably aware of
their existence could very well mean extinction for their kind.
For armies of ravenous new ones to be so carelessly and
thoughtlessly made in such a short time could bring both
worlds to the brink of extinction, one right after the other
within less than a century. This would mean a fight to the
death like no other. This was because even though the human
world was weaker, by percentages there were more of them
and with that, they were tenacious fighters. The vampire
world would be next, but before that happened, they would all
turn on each other in an attempt to survive starvation until
none remained.

Even if humans were kept as cattle, as Pathos had planned,
the blood would grow weaker, tainted and diseased; in both
races, and all would die eventually anyway. *"Death begets
death"* the words played in Jeremy's mind like a banner. Jeremy
doubted that Pathos had thought that far ahead, or if he had,
he had deluded himself that he would be the one with enough
absolute control to master the negatives of any situation. What
hubris. He did not even seem to realize that this plan would be
hastening his own death as well in one fashion or another.

"Should we not try to get to Dmitri and alert him to this threat?" Onyx asked. She had had her own prior dealings with Pathos and was well aware of how treacherous he was.

"The problem is," Jeremy replied, "is that Pathos is almost a second, and that to accuse one so high and powerful without absolute proof could render us all into the Keeper's hands." The truth of this was universally understood by all present, even Mike. "Still, that is clearly really our only option at this point, because we are not strong enough to overpower him and he is powerful enough to spot our guile from a distance." All agreed.

"I never thought in this life that I would be working so hard to save *food* as it were," Aconia laughed almost bitterly

"You're working to save our existence Aconia," Jeremy replied and with that was silent. Aconia did not speak again. She would bide her time for the moment to see which way things would play out.

Jeremy's thoughts wandered back to the safe house and to the dutiful elder who had made it a point to teach him the history of his new people at the beginning of his transition. Morak, who had come from the family Carcescu in the old country, wove the tale for Jeremy's learning.

It is said, he began, that the original one had struck a dark bargain for his existence; to keep his lands with his family name upon them so that they would not be wiped from the face of the earth by time and conquest. Once his fate was sealed, he had wandered about for the better part of two hundred and fifty years on his own; sating his appetite for food, love, creature comforts, and most of all blood. At that point he realized how alone he was in the world. There was no other like him. He was without peer or companionship of any sort.

He decided to remedy his circumstance by taking from among the human race four exceptional warriors over the next two hundred years whom he would adopt as his sons, both for his personal guard and for his own company. The first was his favorite by far, Algar, a great warrior by any measure. Algar was not only a great and fearless warrior, but he had incredible battle sense and an even stronger sense of intuition, which the original one admired. Algar would be his second.

The next was Dvorak, a battle-hardened warrior who would do anything to win at any cost. His methods were sometimes crude and often cruel, but there was no denying their effectiveness. While the Original one admired Dvorak's strength and cunning, he worried about the future in the hands of this one without proper guidance. He would need to reshape Dvorak somewhat, or else he might tip the carefully orchestrated balance of the vampire world in the wrong direction. His inner knowing also told him, that this one would need to be watched, always.

Dvorak considered himself an equal of Algar from the beginning. This was where the struggle between them began. It often seemed that enmity between them would one day break out into open quarrel with little or no provocation. For this reason, the Original one watched over them carefully for a time; unless open warfare should place his whole new race at risk. At the root of the disagreement, Algar felt a certain remorse for the gifts which had been bestowed upon him by his circumstance while alternately Dvorak reveled in them. He looked for any way that he could exploit these new abilities. Anything that had once been human in his character had died long ago with his human existence. Pathos was descended from this house.

Carcescu was next. His line would be the keeper of the histories of his new people. Recording the history of all that had been, and all that was yet to be in The Book of the Law of Houses. The last house was the house of Zuhr. From this house hailed the most battle-hardened warriors and elite guards. This was the line from which Sercan and Saro came. These were the four houses from which the entire vampire race had descended. Algaerius, Dvorak, Carcescu and Zuhr.

Fealty was automatically sworn to the house into which one was born once transition was complete. The only exception to this rule was a pardon from the leader of the current ruling house. At this time, it happened to be the house of Algaerius into which Dmitri had been born.

It is also told that the Original one had been critically wounded in a battle centuries earlier. In order to repair and replenish his physical countenance, he needed to enter a deep and undisturbed sleep, like death itself. He had decreed beforehand, that should this come to pass, each house would rule the vampire race for a period of three hundred years. This would account for twelve hundred human years before he would walk among his own people once again. When he awakened at the end of that time, he would decide which house had handled this responsibility better than the others. That house and its inhabitants would be honored as seconds for all time. The Original one had done this because, try as they might, the four warriors and four houses could not agree on almost anything for almost two and a half centuries.

The house of Dvorak ruled first, and when their time had passed in which chaos and unrestrained bloodshed had reigned, Dmitri had spent a little over half a century restoring a calculated balance in order to protect their existence. Although Dmitri and Pathos had been born several generations apart, their dislike of each other still lurked just below the surface of their respective existences.

Dmitri was just, but he was also known at times to be without pity for even his own kind. This, some believed owed to a partial memory of his human existence. Pathos, for his part always seemed to try and push the outside edge of that boundary, dangerously close to its collapse. For this reason, they avoided contact with each other whenever possible.

The Original one had also created another and darker line as an attaché to the other four. This was the house of the Keepers of the Second Night. The sleep from which one does not wake. This order dispensed ultimate justice unto the vampire race. All vampires knew almost from the day of their birth that to wind up in the hands of the Keeper meant final death with no pardon.

As Jeremy sat lost in his daydream of vampire history, he heard a sudden rush of air behind him and turned to look up seeing a newly made vampire heading for him with teeth bared and eyes glowing—ready and needing to feed. Jaxon moved at light speed and intercepted him. There was a sickening crunch of bone as Jaxon snapped the vampire's neck, and then deftly reached in and pulled his heart from his chest, but before he had finished, another appeared and was headed straight for Mike, the hunger in its eyes unmistakable.

This time Onyx stepped forward, separating the young vampire's head from his body with such precision of movement that it was hard not to be impressed despite the terror of the situation.

"And so it begins," Jeremy announced without dramatic flair. Mike just sat there, shaken, and wondered how long he would survive in this conflict. He didn't give much for his chances in this war, weak and human as he was. He had seen brutality and the results of it in his time, but this defied even those experiences.

Jeremy looked at the two dead corpses at his feet that were beginning to desiccate. In a few more seconds, they would be dry dust blowing in the wind; almost as if they had never existed. He thought he recognized one of them but was not sure. The one, he thought, might be a football player from a rival school, although that really didn't matter now. That world was so far from his grasp and his reckoning at this point, it was like a dream that he was not sure had ever existed.

Killing their own kind was forbidden except in the most extreme circumstances and times of war. He would have much to account for when this was over. Even so, this was a test and a warning; he was sure of that. He could almost hear Pathos laughing silently. Jeremy knew he had to formulate a plan, and quickly. The battle was about to begin.

Jeremy and Jaxon set about creating and fortifying a battle plan to reach Dmitri. If any of them were to survive, this would be their only path. All agreed with this. The twins would function as watch guards and the first and immediate layer of security. Aconia and Onyx would be the second layer of security. Mike would help strategize the logistics of the plan since he had some experience with this. His overall fate would be decided later if he survived that long. Within the next few hours, battle plans were laid, weapons fashioned, and determination fortified. They were ready to proceed. Jeremy would seek a meeting with Pathos to glean more information about his plans and to figure out a clearer path to Dmitri. Jeremy had never met Dmitri but had heard many tales of their leader. He was reputed to be incredibly strong, but fair, which was rare in their world. He hoped he would get the chance to meet him under less fraught circumstances if he survived.

The Meeting

Pathos stood waiting. The man in the long black coat, impeccably tailored as always. The wind was swirling around him almost raising the dust as Jeremy approached.

"So, finally you come when you hear your master's voice," Pathos said with a bit of acrimony.

"I wasn't aware that I had a master," Jeremy threw out to the wind just to irritate the old vampire. Pathos felt such a sudden surge of anger at Jeremy's insolence that he grabbed him with one hand about his neck, raising him high in the air as his dagger like fingernails dug into the flesh of Jeremy's neck, bringing the blood to the surface. The others were hidden in the surrounding foliage watching the exchange. The twins were ready to spring into action to rescue Jeremy, but Mike urged them back and made a sign to the others to stay calm and hold back for just a moment longer.

Pathos finally dropped Jeremy unceremoniously on the ground. Jeremy rubbed his neck where the old vampire's nails had pierced his flesh. Pathos was incredibly strong, due to his age.

"I am trying to be patient with you new one, but you are trying even *my* patience." Pathos said as he licked his fingers, enjoying the taste of Jeremy's blood on his hand.

"My father used to say the same thing," Jeremy croaked the words out.

"Now, how many new thralls have you and Jaxon found for me?"

"That's the thing. We've been having a little trouble with that," Jeremy responded.

"Why so?" Pathos asked with feigned disbelief. "Have you not been given a power that would dominate and quell the resistance of even the most powerful of these weak and hairless humans?" he asked as he nonchalantly picked at his fingernails, probably looking for the last of Jeremy's blood.

"Yes, but trying to take one stealthily with no one around or in such a way that doesn't arouse murderous suspicion is not easy."

"Well, I suggest that you find a way," Pathos countered, "otherwise you'll be of no use to me, and things that are of no use get disposed of." He let the words hang threateningly in the air.

The others began to twitch nervously in the foliage. What they hadn't thought about was that Pathos was already aware of their presence. He had smelled them even before they arrived but didn't want to take the time to deal with them all at the present time. There would be time for that when his other plans had been set into place. "I need at least five new ones by tomorrow eve. If not, your already short life in this world may meet its untimely end."

"Understood," Jeremy replied without contrition or fear in his voice.

"Oh, and as to your little mates hiding in the bushes yonder, that goes for them as well." With this proclamation, Pathos disappeared in a cloud of dust almost as suddenly as he had appeared. They all let out their breath together as one entity, each one wondering separately how they were all going to survive.

After Pathos departed their meeting, Jeremy and the others began talking among themselves, almost forgetting about Mike in the process. Jeremy rubbed his neck where Pathos' nails had cut into his flesh and found that it was already healing. That was the one redeeming factor he found in this new life. Vampires were pretty close to indestructible. Almost. Jeremy addressed the group once again. "There is not time enough to get to Dmitri; we will have to handle this ourselves. The only way I can see to prevent the cataclysmic downfall of our race and all other life is to kill Pathos before he has a chance to enact his psychotic plan."

"Did becoming a vampire remove all your sensibilities as well as your human life?" Aconia asked in disbelief. "Pathos is generations older and many times stronger than we are all together. He will kill us all as easily as a child playing with toy soldiers."

"That may be, however, if we do nothing, or worse yet, try to get to Dmitri and fail, all will be lost without resistance to the insanity he is proposing." Jeremy replied. "I find it preferable to die trying to save what little we have now, rather than letting Pathos plunder and rule both worlds; even if in that undertaking, we are all rendered into the hands of the Keeper." All murmured in agreement somewhat grudgingly. Mike figured he was probably as good as dead anyway.

They had one day to come up with a plan. They started to work. They would fortify their positions and Jeremy would call another meeting with Pathos. While Pathos was otherwise engaged, they would set upon him and try to kill him. They had a slightly better chance all together than if there were only one. If they were successful, they would still all likely be rendered into the hands of the Keeper. Not only for killing one of their own kind, but one so high. Which meant that they would likely be made to suffer greatly before their lives ended. If they were unsuccessful, they would all die anyway, but in the process, Dmitri would become aware of a problem within his ranks and would take action to deal with the situation. Their survival was immaterial, but also not likely whichever way the battle went. Once they had all mentally accepted this, they were ready. Ready to sacrifice their lives in this valiant cause. Mike was along for the ride and realized that his choices in this situation had already been made for him. He was suddenly glad that he had no one to leave behind.

Jeremy paced slowly back and forth in the chilly night air. There was a bit of damp fog finding its way to him, just like in an old movie as he concentrated on trying to home in on Pathos. One of the first things he had learned after becoming a vampire was that a vampire is never truly separated from his or her sire. They are always connected telepathically and are able to communicate in the same fashion; the way he and Jaxon did all the time. Some of their kind were also able to mask or cloak their thoughts. Jeremy was trying to learn this now. Most did not have this ability, but Jeremy was determined that if this ability existed within him at all, he would find it and exploit it to his will. It could very well prove useful in the future he thought. Just as he was becoming discouraged enough to give up, he heard the old vampire's laughter in his mind. It grew louder and louder until it became a deafening roar.

"Oh, silly boy, do you really think that you have the mental dexterity, physical power, or any other means at your disposal to overpower me? Me? The one who made you? What audacity! I would have already done away with you if you did not amuse me so at times. You almost remind me of myself when I was new. I can't say as much for your friends, but I am content to leave them be. For now. I will meet you tomorrow night as previously decided. Don't be late or there will be consequences." Jeremy knew he had no choice but to obey.

Pathos wanted to meet tomorrow, because the day after tomorrow the moon would be full. It was to be a Super Moon giving all the new ones made in that cycle since the last full moon incredible strength, power and agility. Almost three times what they would normally have during a regular cycle.

Jeremy realized all at once that the full moon was when Pathos was planning to launch his coup against Dmitri. He would use his self-made army of super strong, ravenous, blood thirsty ravins to fight the battle. Most seasoned vampires are able to deal with new ones without too much concern, but it is not easy due to the strength and determination of purpose that they possess. It can a challenge to deal with one such vampire, but a whole army? There were only seven of them, Jeremy thought. How would they ever stop an army with only one focus—food?

With this thought, Jeremy ruminated on just how much he had learned about his new life in such a short time. He had adapted with almost lightning speed and seemed to know things instantly, almost more by instinctual sense rather than actual learning. While Jeremy realized that he was progressing faster than most, likely because the part of his human essence which had been able to think around problems had remained with him through transition; he was sure that his transition was still not progressing quickly enough to deal with the approaching situation. He would have to use all the abilities that he currently possessed, and all the determination that he could call upon to try and pull this off. Without that at the beginning, they were all doomed to fail miserably. It made him wish that he had a better plan at this moment. The good thing was that the qualities that had come through transition with him were becoming more acute and more razor sharp every minute. They had become incredibly heightened already; the same way his physical senses had in the beginning. All he could do now was hope that they stood a chance against Pathos. He knew that even if everything worked out with near perfect synchronicity, the chances of prevailing against the old vampire were less than slim. Still, there was hope he thought.

These thoughts took him back to his room at the safe house. As he entered his room, he could sense that something was off. Someone had been there recently. Someone other than those normally there. As he looked around the room, he instinctively sensed a different presence. It was masculine and incredibly powerful. For a moment he thought that Pathos had been there. If Pathos wanted to visit, there were none there that could stop him or offer challenge, including himself. Jeremy walked around the room. Nothing was out of place, yet he could still feel the emanation of the presence. He walked over to the window to look outside at the night darkness as he tried desperately to come up with some sort of plan to save them all.

As he went to open the window to catch the familiar scent of the night breezes, which he found so comforting, he noticed a coal black feather sitting ever so gently and out of place on the windowsill. He picked it up and turned it over in his hand again and again, wondering as to its owner. He knew that whoever this feather belonged to was also the owner of the presence that he felt. He was also fairly sure it wasn't Pathos. Still, with all that he knew about his new world, this was beyond him. He put the feather away to give it further consideration at a later time if he made it back.

The Test of Iron Wills

The next evening, Jeremy set out to meet Pathos as he had been duly ordered. Mike and the others would already be there waiting for Jeremy to arrive and waiting for the appropriate time to present itself; to come to his aid. Jeremy walked in the cool damp evening, air breathing deeply and enjoying the night sounds. The smell of the blooming night fragrances was almost titillating. It was at this point that he felt more than heard the presence behind him. This was not the same presence that had visited his room earlier. This was something else. He turned to see a youth of roughly his same age and stature following him. As he stared roughly twenty yards behind him, the youth stopped. It was another vampire. This he could already tell by the stance, the smell of recent feeding, and the almost overconfident air about him.

This, though, was not a brand new one, although he was only a slightly older than Jeremy. This was a hired gun that Jeremy was sure had been sent to clean up the problem that he and the others were presenting of late. This was also a test to see how battle ready they all were. Suddenly the face hardened, and the eyes took on a red unearthly glow that burned with purpose. He heard the snarl before he saw the face coming at him with fangs unsheathed to do their worst. Jeremy attempted to step aside, but the youth was agile, more agile than Jeremy had counted on. The air left his body in a whoosh as he was tossed into an adjacent building. The experience was painful but not paralytic.

Jeremy regained his footing quickly and brought his full vampire essence to the surface before the next blow landed. His vampire teeth, his razor-sharp nails, his snarl, and most of all his deathly stare. The vampire lunged at him again, but this time he glided out of the way and landed a blow across the vampire's face and neck with his nails, drawing blood and taking flesh with it. This enraged his opponent to the point where he lunged again without taking time to consider his strategy. As he connected with Jeremy, he was pushed against the building and Jeremy sunk his teeth deep into his opponent's neck but did not drink as he normally would have, but instead spit the vampire's blood out onto the ground beside them in a brazen act of self-preservation and an accompanying display of insolence. "Death begets death", Jeremy remembered Jaxon's dire warning. With that thought, Jeremy deftly broke his adversary's left arm to slow him down, hoping that this would deter him from wanting to engage in further battle. It didn't. The vampire howled loudly in pain, fueled by rage. As Jeremy took a step back, the vampire lunged toward him again, wild, snarling, and enraged, and nearly out of control as a result, but this time Jeremy met his opponent quickly driving his hand with razor-sharp nails into his opponent's chest and seizing his heart with a crushing blow and bringing his opponent into the realm of stillness for all time.

There was no malice and no regret in the deed, just acceptance. He stood there momentarily as he watched the life fade from his opponent's eyes; knowing that in a few moments he would turn to ash. It gave him no pleasure to kill one of his own kind. He did not even feel the superiority that one usually feels when they best an opponent. He just knew that he must survive as long as possible if he and the others were to have even a fighting chance of survival. Jeremy continued on, healing as he walked until he reached the backside of the park where the meeting was to take place.

He climbed the muddy bank of the back hill with ease until he crested the grassy berm. As he approached, he could see Pathos standing there all but tapping his watch that he didn't even need to look at. Beside him were four of his newest thralls. They flanked him in a half circle like an oddly strange security detail. It was not immediately clear what stage of transition these vampires were in, but Jeremy could tell that they were all relatively new.

"Young Jeremy," Pathos spoke to the open air as if he were giving an introduction at an award ceremony. "How nice of you to finally join us." Jeremy's face remained impassive as he spoke.

"It's not as if I had another option," he replied bleakly.

"Quite true," Pathos returned in an almost giddy tone. "Now, shall we get down to business? Time is wasting as it were, and I have much to accomplish this evening." Jeremy studied the old vampire to see if he could glean a weakness in him. He was looking for a chink in Pathos' armor that he could penetrate at an opportune time, but he was unable to find any for the moment.

There was also still the other matter of the security detail, but he was thinking that Mike and the others could potentially take these. He knew that Onyx and the twins were battle-hardened. Jaxon could handle himself, and Aconia was apt to be more cunning than battle hardened but was still a force to be reckoned with in her own right. Mike had already been to war, but not like this. He would need to be looked after in as much as anybody could do under the current circumstances. Jeremy had told Mike at their last meeting to stay close to Saro and Sercan no matter what. He hoped that would be enough, but truly, at this point he didn't know.

Pathos spoke first. "The rest of my army should be joining us shortly." Jeremy looked over his right shoulder and saw that the moon was coming up and looking full. There wasn't much time to make a play if one were to be made at all. Like a gambler in a poker game, Jeremy studied every tic of the old vampire, hoping that in one small moment, he would betray a weakness previously undiscovered. More than that, Jeremy was hoping he could trick Pathos into acting without thinking, thus giving him and the others the upper hand even if it were only momentary. It might just be enough to tip the battle in their favor for a second or two and that might be just enough all together. Of course, the likelihood was that they would all die, but he couldn't think about that just now...

Ego seemed to be Pathos' Achilles' heel. He was wanting to constantly talk about how great and how strong he was; how much he knew, how cunning he could be, and most of all how he could spot another's treachery from a distance. As Jeremy thought about this, he realized what his hail Mary play would be. He would challenge Pathos' ego, thereby challenging the vampire as it were. People, and vampires who were once people, were like books. If you knew how to read them, it could provide you with enough insight to possibly level the playing field.

Jeremy looked at Pathos somewhat disinterestedly and said, "So it would appear that you have all the particulars worked out?"

"Of course, I have," Pathos retorted. "As if a boy such as yourself, and a relatively new one at that, would understand anything to do with strategy."

He looked up at Pathos and said, "Not much, it's true, but I do know that if Dmitri should get wind of that strategy, we will all be in the Keeper's hands."

"You let me worry about Dmitri," Pathos growled.

"As you wish," Jeremy said.

"Oh, and boy, see to it that you remember whose bidding it is you are to do. Any deviation from that will bring dire consequences for you and your entourage, and the only Keeper you will need to worry about will be me. You see, you belong to me now. That scar on the back of your right shoulder that looks somewhat like a dagger? It is my blood sign. My mark upon you, sort of like a cattle brand, if you will. All new vampires born into our world, are born with the mark of their sire somewhere on their body. Hence, you are mine. Remember that the next time you're feeling independent. I picked you to be mine because of your abilities and your intelligence. Please don't disappoint me." The cruel smile lit his mouth once again and allowed the cruelty that he was known for to shine forth from him like a beacon.

Jeremy let his thoughts wander just for a moment, back to his childhood and all the simple things he'd known over the last nearly eighteen years. His mother's tender embrace and how she would try to soothe the hurt feelings away that his father had put there every time things went awry with his dad. She desperately wanted him to know that he was loved. His dad's drunkenness and subsequent temper tantrums where he and his mother hid out till his dad passed out, and then the morning after where his dad would cry and apologize over breakfast too many times to count.

There was a little league championship he had won with his teammates at nine. The broken leg at twelve during a football game at the local park with his friends. And the sweetest memory of them all; a girl that he'd had a crush on in his junior year. She was beautiful like an angel, with golden hair and beautiful blue eyes, but she had liked someone else. One of his closest friends; he didn't have many. He had never told her how he felt, and now he never would. All these thoughts passed too quickly through his mind for him to settle on any certain one, but still they reminded him that he had lived once. Even if that existence had been brief. It prepared him for the probability that his life was about to be extinguished for all time. With that he decided that there was no time like the present to enact his hastily constructed plan.

"So, you seem pretty sure of yourself, Pathos," Jeremy let a little insolent chuckle escape his lips.

"You'd do well to mind your manners fledgling and hold your tongue, lest I should take offense and rip it out of your insolent mouth along with your attached heart. That is, if you're fond of your pathetic puny life."

"Oh, I am, but I figure it's about to end one way or another anyway on this battlefield. Either with you or against you. For my part I'm hoping Dmitri gets wind of your battle plans and machinations. Then we'll see if you're really as superior as you claim." Jeremy said this last bit with unmistakable insolence. Pathos' face contorted with rage. "It will be nothing short of amusing to see you in Dmitri's clutches, begging for your life the way you had always hoped that I would beg you for mine...Never..." Jeremy let the last word trail off.

This last display of brazen insolence from Jeremy proved too much for Pathos. He leapt with ferocity; snarling with his vampire teeth bared and his eyes glowing deep red. Jeremy saw the face that everyone had come to know him by; as it fell away until all that was left was a frightening caricature as old and corrupt as time; with a pair of glowing red eyes like a pair of evil crown jewels. He grabbed Jeremy by his throat; snarling and making ready to do the very thing he had promised.

All at once Sercan and Saro appeared. They were both brandishing their weapons ready for battle in a valiant attempt to save their friend and comrade. Sercan swung his sword and Saro brandished a double bit axe. They were determined to protect their friend and chosen leader at all costs. This only further angered Pathos who grabbed Sercan and ran him through with his razor-sharp nails, extracting his heart as if it were a seed pit that had gotten in his way as he rebuffed Saro with a brutal wave of his hand.

He tossed Sercan's heart onto the ground in front of where

Saro lay; his neck and spine broken in three places; his left leg and foot completely mangled at an odd angle. His body had been broken, but not his spirit. He would begin to heal momentarily. At least enough for him to continue the fight. At that very moment, Saro suddenly realized that the only thing that had been broken or breached beyond repair was his heart. The brothers were no more. Saro looked over at Sercan where he lay limp on the ground like a balloon that had suddenly lost air and fallen to earth; coming to rest in the first place he touched down.

Saro dragged his mangled body over to where his brother lay. As he held him, he whispered the songs of long ago in his ear as tears sprang forth from him like a river. Songs of who they had been in childhood and as young warriors. Stories of heroic deeds that had carried them through two lives. How they had saved each other time and again. His tears flowed freely in waves for the other half of him who was now gone. His physical injuries of the moment were nothing compared to that of the heart that he had been so sure no longer existed within him. It was now broken beyond the hope of repair.

They had always been one; two sides of the same coin. They had never been separated by anything, not even death. This had been the way of it since before they were born. He promised Sercan that he would be with him again soon, and that they would once again be as they had always been. As the visions of who they had been, played in Saro's mind like an old film, he prepared himself for his final battle. They had been the warriors of their time and beyond. Saro's grief was overwhelming, making his desire for revenge fierce, like white hot pitted steel and without requite. It was like a fevered sickness that takes one into the next realm. He was ready.

He would stand one last time against Pathos, which he knew would ultimately result in his death for all time, but he and Sercan would be together again. Without his brother, he was utterly lost; beyond caring and unable to exist. He had already accepted his fate, and he was ready to move from this life to whatever awaited him next; as long as Sercan was there. With these thoughts, he stoically pulled himself into a standing position with his weapon ready. He had nearly almost healed from the physical wounds bestowed upon him by Pathos.

Nearby, Jeremy was desperately trying to figure out a way to intervene without getting them both killed, but he was not quick enough. It all happened quickly in what seemed like a fraction of a second. Pathos turned and smiled. It was the wicked smile of one who has no right to be the victor, but who will claim the title, nonetheless. Not because of birthright or nobility, but because of sheer strength and the ability to use brutal force to his advantage. The smile meant to taunt Saro found its mark. Saro returned the smile with an extended arm as he motioned his fingers in a gesture for Pathos to come forward and reap his reward. Saro whirled the double bit ax above his head in a display of fierce challenge. He wanted Pathos to see that he was unafraid. The sound of the whirring blades was almost hypnotic as Saro rushed toward Pathos heatedly. His only thought and purpose at that moment was to avenge his brother's death. As he attempted to sink his blade through Pathos' midsection and connect with the lower end of his heart, Pathos deflected Saro's blade with a wave of his arm, but the blade caught Pathos' upper left arm in the process which began to bleed steadily. Pathos screamed; enraged by the wound given to him by one that he considered so insignificant. This was evident in the trill of his voice. Saro smiled, returning the taunt as he looked back into the face of his own demise. It was a smile of pure hatred, burgeoning with the promise of a violent death to follow for the one who failed. Saro lunged again. This time Pathos stepped deftly out of the way and grabbed Saro as he attempted to adjust his trajectory. It was the mistake that would cost Saro his life. Pathos reached back and snapped Saro's left shoulder as he plunged his other fist through the middle of his back, closing his fist around Saro's heart and pulling it from his body. In one last cruel gesture he showed Saro his heart before he crushed it into dust before him, sprinkling the ground with the dusty remains and brushing his hands off as if it had all been so effortless. He reveled in the supremacy he felt as he danced around, cloaking himself in it. Saro smiled victoriously as the last of his life force left him. His promise had been kept and he could now rest. He was free for all time.

Jeremy felt broken and stunned in one motion. He felt as if half of his life force had just been ripped from him in one moment. He ran. Pathos looked around for Jeremy not finding him. This served to rekindle his anger once more. Jeremy had run away as soon as he had witnessed Saro's death at Pathos' hand. He did this knowing he could do nothing to help or save his friend at that point. He ran for whatever cover he could find and to buy time. When he finally found the others, he sat shaking among them like a leaf on a tree in the wind of a gathering storm. He was not sure what twist of thought had convinced him he that had even had a chance of prevailing against Pathos in any arena. He thought about this as he wrestled with a terrible overwhelming guilt, believing that he had gotten Sercan and Saro killed trying to protect him. There was also another part of him that was smoldering with a molten hatred toward Pathos. That part of his consciousness wanted only retribution. His anger was so strong; it almost breathed with a life of its own. It would not let him find the focus he so desperately needed now to plan his next move.

Onyx stepped up to act as Jeremy's protector and body-guard for the time being now that the twins had been eliminated. Jaxon would always be Jeremy's second. This had already been decided without words when they had bonded weeks ago at the beginning of Jeremy's transition, but Onyx would still watch after him for the time being. At least until this current crisis had been averted.

As he sat there with all these thoughts swimming through his mind, Jeremy hung his head in shame, not wanting to look at the others. By his reckoning, he figured that they must all blame him too, or should. Onyx was the first to speak.

"There is nothing that you could have done," she said quietly. "The twins knew the risk of this undertaking, as we all do. In battle, some don't return. We all know that this is the reality of this life and that this is the mother of all battles."

"I didn't expect them to come to my aid," he said miserably, almost choking on the words. "I thought I could handle Pathos and his threats."

"Experience is often a dear teacher. Do not let your anger be your keeper; for it will fail you," she responded quietly and then walked over to the others.

The others milled around trying to decide what to say or do next. After a bit, they all then came forward one by one, murmuring their condolences and affirming their promise to follow Jeremy to the end of this undertaking. They were still all of the same purpose and still all solidly behind Jeremy. A stray tear which should not be there because vampires don't feel emotion the way that humans do, escaped briefly and slid silently down Jeremy's cheek. It became the water of life that sealed their bond with each other for all time.

THE LAST WORD

Jeremy traced his steps back to where the battle had taken place and Sercan and Saro had lost their lives. It would be dawn soon and time to retreat and rest up for the next evening when the moon would be full, and the fight would be on in full regalia. Jeremy didn't even have much of a battle plan, but he would try to construct one in the few short hours he had left. At least for the others if for no one else. He couldn't knowingly let them down, even if he ultimately failed.

His heart was heavy with the knowledge that they had not been able to reach Dmitri in time, but he hoped that as word of the battle traveled, they could slow Pathos down enough to allow time for Dmitri to intervene and put a stop to his insane plans. He truly didn't know if all his efforts had been in vain, but he hoped not. He could see the gray light on the horizon getting ready to usher in the day. It was time for sleep and then the final night would be upon them.

Jeremy awoke at dusk and Mike settled down for a short cat nap. He had stood guard through the day while the others slept well hidden within the reaches of an old, abandoned building on the edge of town. The safe house was no longer safe. As Mike settled into a light fitful slumber, the others began to discuss plans, strategies, and possible contingencies. After almost an hour of this, they were ready.

Mike began to dream vividly of war, blood, and fire until he was thrashing about violently. There were images of people he had saved on the battlefield and those he couldn't. There was Aunt Dona pleading with him about things long forgotten and then there was Pathos, laughing at all of it. The others watched Mike sleeping, which served to illustrate for each one of them that this would be anything but easy, whichever way it went.

Jeremy roused Mike a little while later. Mike came to groggily.

"You can stay here," Jeremy said without emotion. "This isn't your fight, it's ours, and there's no sense in you risking your neck to save vampire life as we know it."

"I thought I was risking my life for the human component," Mike returned.

"Either way, if you die, we die and vice versa at this stage of the game. Besides, I know you didn't ask for this."

"Neither did you," Mike responded.

"True enough," Jeremy said, "but I still feel that this is more our fight than yours."

"Well, either way, I'm coming along."

"Suit yourself," Jeremy replied as he stared off into the distance, wondering exactly what the next few hours would bring and who would emerge the victor. He already had a pretty good idea about that, though.

The group gathered their gear and their weapons together and trudged off in the direction of the wilderness area of the park. Each was lost in his or her own thoughts as they walked silently forward. For some reason, that venue seemed to be the fulcrum of this event. It was where all the major components of this drama had already taken place, and it seemed to be the place where the rest would finally be decided. Jeremy could see the bright pale moon beginning to rise high in the sky. It wouldn't be long now...

As they walked, Jeremy's mind wandered into the past again. He remembered the simplicity of life as it used to be before he became a vampire. The holiday parties; his friends and the dumb jokes they used to tell; running around town getting into and out of trouble; staying one step ahead of the law and their parents. He only wished that his choices were that simple now. It made him sad to think that it had all passed away without him ever really appreciating it.

HISTORIES

Aconia had been the daughter of the local Apothecary, born Margaret Anne Milshire. She was headstrong, beautiful, and slightly dangerous even before becoming a vampire, but her induction into this world only served to enhance those qualities, if anything. She would often laugh and play jokes and run about town with her friends. The high-born society of town would look down their noses at her disapprovingly because of her wild ways. This had led to more than one row with her parents, who would implore and cajole her to behave and settle down so that she might find a suitable husband and take her place in decent society. She wanted none of that right now. She wanted only her freedom from the constraints of this life; the expectations and traditions. She was still young. There would be plenty of time to settle down later. Right now, she just wanted to live as much as she could.

After one such episode with her parents, one night her journey began. That night she met a handsome dark stranger at one of the local dances. He was visiting family and would be in town for a few weeks during the summer season. It was like a whirlwind. One dance led to another and another until one night he asked if he could walk her home. They talked on and on as they had for the past week. His name was David Marshall, and he was here visiting his aunt who lived in a modest home at the end of town. Margaret was sure she had met the woman, but for some reason couldn't recall her at the present time. Oh well, she was sure she would be formally introduced to her soon enough and then all would fall into place and come clear.

On the way home she became rather sleepy and didn't remember much after that except that she woke up in a strange bed, with the sun streaming in through the windows and she suddenly felt sick and weak and tired. Something was very wrong. The sun felt like a knife cutting into her skull and all she wanted to do was sleep. There was also a strange wound on her right shoulder that she couldn't remember getting. She wondered if it had something to do with the sickness she was feeling now. She vomited and then succumbed to the blackness that was sleep. As she slept, she dreamt of David. He was holding out his hand to her, telling her that everything would be alright. He told her he would take her away from this dreary life and the lack of what it had to offer her and take her to a new place where she would be revered as a queen. She had only to take the drink that he held out to her, and her journey would begin. She took the liquid and drank it. It tasted slightly bitter and a bit metallic, but she began to feel much better almost instantly.

She noticed that she preferred sleeping during the day and that she would have vivid dreams of David while she slept; always bringing that liquid and offering it to her to drink. One night she awoke during one of these dreams and David was standing there in her room. It was as if he had been standing over her, watching her sleep until she awoke. He held out his hand to her and bade her come with him. She was momentarily stunned that he should be there at all. It was at the very least highly improper. Where were her parents? He explained that she had fainted the previous evening on the way home and that he had brought her to his aunt's home to recover.

She was worried about what her parents would say about all this. She had never stayed away from home over night before and certainly not with a strange man. He told her that his aunt was overseeing all the proprieties and that she needn't worry. He also told her that he had sent a servant to her parents' house to let them know what had happened. Margaret was momentarily satisfied with this explanation.

A short time later, David came once again to her room as she was making ready to leave and go home to face the disapproval of her parents. He told her that they should take a walk so that he could further explain the situation as it was. As they walked in the cool evening air, he did just that—explained. Explained who and what she was now and why she could never go back home. At first, she thought he must be trying to play a horrible joke on her or that he was truly raving mad. She stood there in stunned disbelief for a moment not wanting to believe what he was saying but feeling the very truth of it at her core. She began to cry in horror and to beg for him to put her back the way she had been. He told her that he could not and that she would adjust in time. She wailed.

He also told her that the world she had just been born into had given her a new name. Aconia: short for Aconite or Night-shade. She was his beautiful midnight flower. His real name was Pathos, and then he told her to make ready quickly as they had a long journey ahead of them. As she sat there crying, she wondered how she would ever survive this. It was at that moment that she dried her tears as the hardened and deter-mined part of her character stepped forward and took its place at the helm of who she was now. She was determined that she would somehow make Pathos pay for what he had done to her and for what he had taken from her.

She wished at that moment that she could tell her parents how very much she loved and missed them, and how sorry she was for all her misbehavior, but she knew that this was all past now as she made ready for the journey. There would be time to settle accounts later she thought bitterly. She had no intention of giving up or giving in until that happened. Tomorrow was another day; or night as it were in her case now.

Jaxon Bedford had been the well-to-do favored son of a local politician and tax collector; not to mention Lane County's most eligible bachelor. He had never wanted for anything. The family he hailed from were not quite rich, but they were more than comfortable. There were friends and society parties with no shortage of beautiful girls vying for his attention. Most of them were wanting to marry well and settle into a comfortable life, with a rich if not handsome husband from a well-to-do family, if possible. Jaxon's looks would be solace enough if they could not convince him to love. That, and there were always other pursuits for company if need be....

He did have a particular favorite among all the girls trying to catch his eye; her name was Moira Rose Gildean. She had beautiful porcelain skin with light brown hair and beautiful hazel eyes. When she laughed it sounded like little musical bells. She was always smiling, and he had never heard her say a cross word to or about anyone. She was warm and kind and he could see the makings of a fine wife and mother in her character. It would be a fitting match one day, but there was time enough for that he thought.

Jaxon had not counted on one thing, though; the party he would attend that night and the after party of sorts which would follow. That party was where he would meet David Marshall, a well-to-do entrepreneur and shipping tycoon up-start of modest means who would talk on and on late into the night about other people's money and how to best make it work for them. It seemed he had an uncle who was well to do and who would finance him and a partner who had the ability to bring business sense to bear...

A couple of days later, Jaxon woke up with the hangover of

his life and learned that he would never return to the life he had once led. He was now a servant to Pathos, a vampire who had many plans; the least of which was letting Jaxon lead his own life. Moira, with the voice like musical bells would be only a sweet memory now. Such was life, or as it was now...death.

Jaxon lay in a depression for days, not eating and barely sleeping, but only in daylight hours. He was trying to figure a way out of this trap, but at last he realized that there was none. At least none that he could effect on his own right now. He settled into being a manservant for the time being to Pathos, but he vowed to himself that one day, when the opportunity presented itself, that he would be ready and at the very least would attempt to exact revenge for the injustice done to him.

This arrangement continued for many years until such time as Pathos decided that Jaxon had settled into his new life well enough for the most part, and set him somewhat free, but not too free. He cautioned Jaxon to be ready when he heard his master's call...

The next time Pathos called was when he turned Jeremy. Jaxon felt a certain empathy for Jeremy having been in the same situation himself almost a century earlier. The two became fast friends, and Jaxon realized their destinies were tied tightly together. How closely he never could have imagined.

Onyx had been the jewel of her father's eye from the moment she was born. A midwife had announced the birth of a baby girl which had been foretold by the elders for many years. A black Queen who would be born among them to whom others would bow, under the power of her sword and her wisdom. She was aptly named Onyx for the blackest stone of the strongest character which held the sharpest edge. She grew stronger and more beautiful each day from the moment she was born, and she was a delight to behold. She seemed to inspire enchantment wherever she went. The elders also told of a shadow cast across the day of her birth, a dark spot in her future between her seventeenth and nineteenth year. It was a small mark, but present, nevertheless. If she were fortunate and the fates smiled kindly upon her as they had done at her birth and she did not anger them through the younger years of her life, she might escape whatever shadow the dark mark held.

She was educated by both elders and by wise men; not to mention the most skilled warriors the land had to offer. One day during her eighteenth year, she was off exploring, as she was known to do from time to time. Her father always urged her to take a guard detail with her whenever she went out and about, because he was afraid of what the dark mark held, but she was unafraid. She could best almost any man or woman with a sword or without one. As skilled as she was with a sword, her real power was her wisdom and intelligence. After all, she had been taught by the best generals in the land.

As she rounded the next bend, she saw a small riding party of three. There was a man on horseback who was clearly the leader of the group and the other two in tow were obviously servants in some capacity. One was Jaxon whom she would come to know in much more detail later on. As she drew nearer still yet unseen, she heard the group's leader speaking to the other two in a harsh, almost gritty voice, chastising them for some infraction they had obviously committed. He was tall and dark, with pale skin. He was extremely good looking with eyes like the color of tiger agates.

He was clearly of another land. Most of those from her land had dark skin like hers. He was dressed oddly as well, not like the other people in her city, nor any other she had ever been to. One of the servants, the one called Jaxon, also had fair skin. His hair was the color of straw, and his eyes were blue like the morning sky.

She had only seen a man with such lovely white skin one other time in her life. It was when she visited the city of Suldien. She had traveled there to meet the one she was betrothed to. It had been a week-long ceremonial feast complete with dancing, proclamations, and prayers as was the custom in her part of the world. Within the year she would be wed to the heir of that city and would take her rightful place as his queen. Until then, however, she would explore and enjoy her freedom before she was charged with the duties of state and childbearing as was the custom for women of her time and station. Her mind wandered back to that time with all of its bright colors and ceremony.

Suddenly, the strange man stopped speaking as if he sensed her presence. Onyx all at once had this prickly feeling all over her skin and then it vanished.

"Hello, is there someone there? Come forward, won't you? We mean you no harm." he called out in softened tones. Gingerly, she stepped forward from her hiding place, trying to assess the situation as she went. She stepped forward without fear as she was confident that she could protect herself should that become necessary. The leader of the group introduced himself as Umbra, a merchant from the city of Sommeran.

He told her he had traveled a great distance to her land. "It is many days' journey from here," he told her. She raised an eyebrow imperceptibly as her curiosity was aroused. The time of year was still early as most of the first merchants would not arrive for another two to three months by her count and her memory.

"What have you brought to sell?" she asked.

"Spices, silks, and jewelry to grace the beauty of one such as yourself, as well as a few special trinkets."

"What trinkets?" she asked innocently curious. He made a gesture for her to wait there for just a second and with that he disappeared into a small tent that had been recently pitched when he and the others made camp. He returned a moment later with two boxes. One was very small, about the size of an orange and the other was somewhat larger. He opened the larger one first and took out a silver chain with an odd medallion attached. It was shaped like a very small dagger, about the length of her forefinger with three loops for a handle. The first loop held the silver chain that was threaded through it. The other two loops held two beautifully cut stones. One was blood red and the other a deep violet color.

"M'lady, I present to you the world's smallest dagger. Consider this my gift to you, for your protection." He obviously didn't realize how capable she already was of protecting herself and she smiled at the thought. Still, she decided that she would play along for now until she could determine his true intention. Besides, she was quite taken by this unique piece of jewelry.

"May I?" he asked as he held up the necklace in a gesture indicating that he wished to place it around her neck.

She stood still while he placed the chain around her neck and fastened the clasp. Next, he offered her the smaller box about the size of an orange. She took it from him and curiously lifted the lid. Sweet music began to play, and she smiled with delight as she listened. She had no way of knowing at the time that this was the last innocent moment she would know. Umbra asked her to dine with him and his two servants that evening. She felt she could hardly refuse his request after he had presented her with two such lovely gifts. He looked at her beyond the guile of his eyes and thought about how delectable she looked right at that moment.

They dined into evening and talked of many things. Umbra was charming and the conversation stimulating. The two servants hung back, watching. She noticed that the blonde one's eyes seemed to keep shifting around as they followed her. This piqued her curiosity and her wariness.

Just about that time, she began to feel sleepy, almost more tired than she could ever remember. As the night closed in around her, she heard Umbra's voice whispering not to worry, that everything would be just fine in a little while. When she awoke, she felt groggy, as if she had been drugged and her head ached like it was on fire. Her right shoulder hurt fiercely. She reached up to touch the source of the pain and saw the crimson ribbon of her own blood as she pulled her hand away.

She looked around and there was no one there. She could not remember anything other than becoming extremely sleepy while she was having dinner with Umbra and his servants, but even that memory was hazy. It was almost as if she had imagined the whole thing, but her wounds were real. It was dark and beginning to get cold. An early breeze had begun to blow. She reached up and felt the tiny dagger around her neck, which told her that her experience had been real. She must get help. She must get to the healer and her father. She rose unsteadily to her feet and instantly careened into a nearby rock formation. Using it to steady herself, she pushed off it and attempted to stand under her own power. She took several small steps before the blackness closed in on her again.

When she awoke the second time, it was twilight just before dawn. She still felt sick and weak and injured, but she was sure that she could manage to get home. She now wished she had heeded her father's request and taken a guard detail with her. She walked slowly for what seemed like hours. The short journey that should have taken her a little over an hour under normal circumstances took three because of her injuries. When she reached the outskirts of a village near her city, she sensed something out of place. It was nothing she could visually determine at that distance, but more of a sense or a feeling.

As she approached the gates to enter, she noticed that there was no sentry on duty. This was odd because there was always a sentry there, sometimes two. She crept through the gate and looked around. The streets appeared to be deserted. There was an unnatural quiet in the air. Fear was beginning to find its way into her belly. She began to run from house to house; looking for someone, anyone who could help her and tell her what had happened. She entered the first house she came to. It was empty. The second was the same. Then, when she came to the third house and entered, she saw a wave of bloody destruction. The inhabitants all looked as if they had been drained of every drop of blood in their bodies. Their eyes were fixed wide open with terrified expressions on their faces. All of them were dead. What depraved monster could have done this? She wondered hysterically.

She began running from house to house and finding either nothing or finding the same destruction that she already had. She sat down on the floor of the last house she entered and began to cry. She must get home and quickly. This village must have been sacked while she was gone and whoever had not run away had been brutally killed. She just sat there on the floor for several hours, trying to process what had happened and wondering what to do next. The sun was beginning to set, and she was about to rise and attempt to make her way to the next town when she looked up to see a familiar shadow standing in the doorway. It was Umbra.

"My dear," he said, "what must have happened here? It looks as though they were set upon unawares."

"Some foul creature did this," she responded through her tears. "Something unholy."

"Something unholy indeed," he mused quietly. "Come my dear, we must get you to the next town, where they can provide you with help," he reasoned quietly.

"But my family, I have to see if they survived."

"I haven't seen anyone among the living here with the exception of yourself..." he trailed off.

"My city is less than half a day's journey from here," she intoned. "There is one more small village before we reach there."

"Well then, by all means, we must be off without delay," he chirped.

The sun was setting as they began their journey. Onyx gingerly asked Umbra if he knew what had befallen her. He told her that she had fainted the night before while they were dining. He said that he had gone to his tent to retrieve some medicine to help her and that when he had returned, she was gone. He said that he had searched and searched and was not able to find her until he came upon her in this village.

She thought about this and was unable to make sense of it clearly because she was still foggy both from her injuries and all that had happened. As she looked around her in the impending darkness, she saw the blonde servant staring at her intently, as if he knew what had happened, but was not allowed to say or speak of it. She would make it a point to corner him later and wring the truth from him, by force if necessary. She looked back at Umbra, managing a halfhearted smile as she turned to follow him.

She rode in the carriage along the dusty roads, not recognizing much, but grateful that they were headed toward her home. Suddenly, the carriage stopped without warning. Umbra came to her and told her that one of the horses had thrown a shoe and that there was some other problem with the wagon which had caused the whole incident. They would need to camp here for the night and then make their way forward the next day when it was cooler, and all had been restored.

She began to feel uneasy about this and asked him if there were no possible way that they could continue. He assured her that there was not, and that it was best to stop for now until he could make the necessary repairs. She conceded. Again, the blonde servant was studying her intently. This one she was beginning to believe would either be her strongest ally or her worst enemy. She was not sure which one yet, but she was determined to find out soon.

Onyx woke at dusk the next evening. She was feeling much improved from the day before and had almost forgotten about her wound. The traumatic events of the day before seemed less for the moment than they had been. She did however, become almost immediately aware of the acute hunger gnawing at her belly. She must set out and find some food. This would be the first order of business. Everything else could wait until that had been attended to.

She heard a loud whinnying from the horses as if they were in distress. She set out in that direction. The scene she came upon next was one that she was completely unprepared to find. Both servants were engaged in drinking the blood of one of the animals, draining it completely of its life force. She was instantly horrified and continued to watch the scene with a curious morbid fascination. As she was about to creep away without being seen, the blonde servant turned around and looked at her directly, as if he had been aware of her presence all along.

It was at that moment she became aware that she could smell the animal's blood. The smell drove her hunger into a near frenzy. They bade her come near. As she did, she looked into the icy blue eyes of the blonde servant. He stepped back so that she could drink. Fearfully, she began to tremble, knowing that resisting the obvious was futile. She drank deeply; gorging herself until her hunger was sated. Wiping her mouth of the traces of blood she had just consumed, she staggered away in shame and horror. She was a monster. A night terror come to life with no escape from her fate now that she had stepped into the shadow of death.

She let out a cry loud enough to be carried on the wind throughout the valley. It was a howl of indescribable anguish that emanated from the center of her being as she sank into the dirt of the night earth. The tears which could not make her clean again coursed down her cheeks like two separate rivers. She felt a firm hand on her elbow urging her to rise to her feet. She blinked and looked up through her tears; it was the manservant with the straw-colored hair and the eyes like sky. He helped her gently to her feet and walked her over to a rock outcropping near where the animal they had just fed on lay. The manservant looked into her eyes and said, "I know that this is distressing. It was the same for me when I first began to change."

"But, but how?" she asked. "What is to become of me? How do I explain this to my family, my people?"

"You will not have to. All will become clearer in a few days. Meanwhile, you must eat to survive. Either that, or you will fade and eventually die."

"My name is Jaxon, and I will help you."

"But where is Umbra?"

"He is away attending to other matters. Whatever you do, do not vex him unnecessarily, for he has the ability and the desire to bring more of your tears to life than you ever knew you had," he said this last bit in an urgent and dire tone. She took his counsel earnestly.

The next evening, Pathos explained Onyx's new life to her and told her his real name. He told her that he had created her to be his attaché of sorts. She would be a counterpart to Jaxon in his household. While they would not always live under the same roof, she must always be at the ready if he were to call upon her. She was now a Queen of midnight.

She asked about her family and her city. Jaxon looked away as Pathos told her rather abruptly and brutally that they were no more. Her anguished cry reached his ears, and while he felt sorry for her, he was unable to show her any sympathy or help her in front of Pathos. He knew that to do so would have made her lot invariably worse than it already was. As Pathos walked away from Onyx in her misery, Jaxon came forward and bade her come with him. As they walked toward a small, wooded area, Jaxon turned to look at her and told her that he would help her in the survival of this new world. He would teach her all that she would need to know. As a last bit, he told her that he understood her grief, but that she must put all of that away in the box Pathos had given her a day earlier.

"Feelings are only chains to our kind and will place you in harm's way quickly," he said. "They will fade with time, but for the moment, they will have the half-life of your human existence."

The only thing she could feel at that moment was a desire for revenge and one day, if fate allowed, she was determined that she would have it. All these thoughts ran through her mind as the group walked together toward whatever fate had in store for them. She only hoped she would still be alive the following evening.

BATTLE

As they neared the park wilderness area, there was a slight smell of acrid smoke that hung in the air. Jeremy realized that Pathos and his entourage must have lit a fire or two for maximum effect. The air was cold and damp and there was the feeling that death was walking alongside them all. Jeremy turned to Mike, "Stay here and wait for us old man, you won't last five seconds in the middle of what we're headed into, and I can't watch out after you. If one or more of us return, you will be safe, you have my word. If not, try to get away as fast as you can and live to fight another day. I know that isn't much, but it's all I have to leave you with right now." Mike murmured his understanding and stayed back, hidden in the foliage, trying to figure out how to help the group even though he knew that all was probably lost anyway. He tucked himself away to hide from the shadow of the moon that would expose him and think.

The group crested the hill, looking all around them, then up ahead. They could see Pathos standing there waiting. His minions flanked around him like an elite guard. Behind them there were two more rows of hungry new ones standing at the ready. As they neared the pack, Jeremy turned around to look at the others.

His voice was clear and strong as he spoke. "No matter what happens here tonight, know that I have never doubted any of you. You are my brothers and sisters in arms, and I will take you with me wherever tonight leads all of us. Be strong and do not waiver, no matter the outcome. We may not have lived long, but they will know that we were, no matter what happens here tonight."

"For Sercan and Saro!" they all cried out in unison with weapons raised high in a show of solidarity. With that, Jeremy climbed the last hill ahead of the rest of the group to come face to face with Pathos.

"So fledgling, it would seem that you have chosen your own path after all. Not a smart move on your part, but then I cannot expect intelligent reasoning on the part of one so new. Regardless, it will make no difference to your fate." Pathos said as his eyes were beginning to burn with fierce indignation and anger as they narrowed like a cat's.

"You are correct, I have chosen my own path, because yours is completely flawed, but your hubris will not allow you to see it. Besides, if I have to die for what I believe in while trying to thwart an ill-advised, poorly designed plan such as yours, then I am ready. I would sooner die at your hand as a failure, then at Dmitri's as a traitor to my own kind. Either to those I came from or those to whom I belong now." With this, Jeremy was silent. He was willing his mind link with Pathos to work. Pathos began to laugh bitterly.

"Still trying to read my thoughts, fledgling? It seems that I am not the only one guilty of hubris," he laughed louder. What Pathos did not realize was that Jeremy was using his old human abilities that he remembered to read Pathos' external tics and body language to determine his next move. Much like a poker player with a much bigger prize at stake...

Pathos looked from one to another of them all and smiled ruefully as the others joined Jeremy.

"Ah, Onyx, my beautiful ebony Queen, it would appear that you have strayed from my clutches as well, into the errant path of young Jeremy here. Tsk, tsk, what a shame," he droned on with over dramatic flair as if he were performing in a community theater. "Tis no matter, as you have chosen young Jeremy, you will meet your fate with him as well. I see that you are still wearing the token I gave you when we first met. I am touched he said with a laugh. Just to let you know that dagger that you wear about your beautiful ebony neck is my sigil. My mark upon you, although you should also have a scar that looks relatively the same but more like a birthmark on the back of your right shoulder." Onyx's anger kindled at Pathos' taunt.

"I will use this dagger around my neck to take the life from you if I get half the opportunity," she threw back at him. He laughed delightedly.

"Ooh and the party would not be complete without Aconia, my beautiful flame haired goddess. You know Aconia, you can still cast your lot in with me. I would never turn away the chance to possess such a beautiful mate," he said with just a little too much fervor for her to remember her manners.

"I would rather be fed to the dogs," she returned.

"And so you shall be," Pathos snarled. "I would never want a mate with so little loyalty as you. The dogs are better than you deserve."

"And last, but not least, Jaxon, my most unloyal servant. What am I to think? I leave you in charge of my estate as my second and you betray me?" he almost strangled on the words. "How dare you! After all that I have given you; you would betray me like this? For a new one?" the anger in Pathos' voice clearly visible and nearly shaking the ground on which he stood.

"No Pathos, I betrayed you for me, whom you tricked with no regard and without asking. For Aconia, whom you tried to enslave as your unwilling mate. For Onyx, whom you cruelly tricked into following you with no mercy, and for Jeremy to whom I pledge my loyalty; whom you cruelly inducted into this world to make use of his talents. How dare you!" Jaxon shouted back. "We are few, but we will stand against you. It is our hope that we can stop you long enough to foil your plan and maybe save all that we once loved, even if we cannot save ourselves."

Pathos began to clap his hands as he laughed "Bravo, bravo" I think you should get an academy award Jaxon, but the hour is late, and I have other things to get to." With that being said, I think we should get on with it. Without further delay, Pathos waved his hand at the two waves of new ones behind him, urging them forward. They rushed forward like a hurricane toward the four. The battle was on.

Mike huddled in the bushes listening, hearing and feeling miserably frustrated; knowing that he had neither the power nor the strength to save his cohorts. He hung his head in shame and tried not to think about the horrible brutal deaths that they would soon be put to and that he would be put to once they found him. To him it almost didn't matter as much as he had no one to leave behind.

As he was becoming lost in these thoughts, he heard a familiar crackling of twigs and branches, but when he looked up expecting to see Jeremy, but it was not Jeremy he saw. It was a giant of a man who reached down and grabbed him with one hand and lifted him off the ground. He knew by instinct and by the breastplate among other accouterments of the man's wardrobe that this must be someone of the vampire world.

He was right, because just as he was attempting to adjust his bearings, the giant looked him over the way a wolf would look at a rabbit and opened his mouth in a giant smile, but it was not a smile. He was baring his teeth as if he were readying himself to feed. Mike closed his eyes preparing himself for the worst. He began to struggle instinctively without screaming, because that would have used energy that he could not afford to spare right at that moment, much less would have been useless at this point.

Just as he was sure he would feel the bite of those razor-sharp canines, he heard a loud thundering voice. It was louder than anything he could remember hearing in a long time. Since the war he had been in. It said "Wait!" and the voice shook the ground upon which they were standing. Mike opened his eyes to see an individual bigger than the one who held him in his grasp; with giant raven-colored wings and raven black hair to match; complete with a forelock. He was strong, muscular and vital. He was quite obviously a force to be reckoned with; the very sight of which could strike fear into the hearts of man or beast. A king not of this world, and clearly not one with whom one should trifle. Dmitri!

"Greetings," he said in a masculine almost booming voice even though he was nearly whispering. "I apologize for the rough treatment you have received at the hand of my second. He means you no harm."

"My apologies," the giant who held him said and set him back down on the ground.

"I am Dmitri," the raven one announced, "and this is Sjoren, my second. We are attempting to reach some of our comrades, and we believe you can help us understand what has happened. Do you know of the disagreement between Pathos and Jeremy?"

"Yes," Mike said, and with that he began to tell the tale for Dmitri who listened enrapt, hanging intently on every word. When he was done with the story, Dmitri's face grew dark, as if a smoldering storm were gathering there. He thanked Mike for his help and directed Sjoren to set him free. He told Mike that they would need to talk again later for obvious reasons, but for now he was free to go. Mike watched as Dmitri and Sjoren took to the blackened sky toward the battlements. Mike hoped that they would be able to reach the others in time.

The battle was already in full swing, and the small group

was rapidly losing ground. Their skills were superior, but their numbers were clearly lacking. Weapons were clashing and some hand-to-hand combat was taking place as well. Pathos was sitting back, watching the show as if it were an evening's entertainment constructed purely for his benefit. The new ones which had rushed the four seemed to be without fatigue. They just kept coming. The four formed a circle with their backs to each other and continued to fight. Each had sustained many wounds from the fight that were in a constant state of healing. They had not been fed on yet. This was because even the new ones dared not disobey Pathos no matter how much their hunger called them or risk a worse fate than what he had already planned for the four.

"Bravo, bravo," Pathos taunted, clapping his hands. He waved away the new ones with his hand and they stopped all at once and stood still. The four stopped and gradually turned around to face the real monster they were battling. They were bruised and battle worn, but still ready to fight to the end which they all knew would soon be upon them.

"You fledglings fight well. It is too bad that you do not know how to serve your master," Pathos drawled.

"Our master is not you," Jeremy shot back.

"Your master will be the grave instead of the everlasting life that I tried to give you all. I will be your Keeper, because you are all traitors of one sort or another and cannot be trusted to do as you are told." There was a moment of silence as the four readied themselves to meet their fate. They looked back and forth at one another silently saying their goodbyes and then they were ready. As they closed their eyes in preparation to meet their fate, there was a loud crack of thunder and two joined their circle. The two largest and most powerful vampires that Jeremy or any of the others had ever seen. Both with large wings dressed in breastplates, complete with armor and weapons.

The one none of the others knew. His hair was a dirty blond color and he had large dark brown wings and was clearly muscular with an obvious chiseled strength about him clearly made for battle. The other needed no introduction. Although none of the four had ever formally met him, they all knew who he must be. The King, Dmitri. Jeremy immediately noticed the raven-colored feathers of his wings and realized it must have been Dmitri who visited his room at the safe house. He felt honored and in awe of the strength and power before him for just the briefest second. Pathos suddenly looked more ashen than his normal countenance.

"The only traitor I see here is you," Dmitri's voice thundered. "You would attempt to enact a plan that would wipe out our race in one fashion or another in order to usurp power that was never yours to begin with, and this goes to prove why it should never be."

"My liege, you misunderstand," Pathos mewled. "I was attempting to thwart the plan of these fledgling traitors... They would have seen the destruction of us all..."

"Hold your fervor Pathos, I believe none of what you say, for I have been watching you from a distance for some time with all of your vile machinations and trickery. I tried to look the other way for a time, but you have betrayed your house and your kind," Dmitri thundered. "This will not stand. Not while I rule."

"I, unlike you, was trying to claim our rightful place in the world," Pathos growled. "I am tired of hiding in shadows and pretending that we don't exist, when we are clearly the superior species." Pathos countered in a bitter tone.

"It is this careful existence that has allowed our kind to survive for thousands of years and not to be constantly at war with humans, who could very well have a chance of overwhelming us if the circumstances were ever tipped in their favor by the natural world. There is also the matter of their tenacity. They are like the badger. Fierce beyond reason when provoked into a fight for their survival. Too many would die on both sides. No matter, you will not have another opportunity after this night. You shall be rendered into the hands of the Keeper, where you should have been sent the day you were born," Dmitri finished acrimoniously. Pathos turned more ashen still and then a slow creeping rage began to surface that became evident on his face.

"In addition to your appointment with the Keeper, the house of Dvorak shall be dissolved, and its inhabitants will be absorbed into the remaining houses," Dmitri continued.

"You can't!" Pathos screamed. "You do not have the authority to make such a decision! The law says that there must be four houses in all."

"Oh, but I do," Dmitri replied calmly.

"You see, as the current ruler of our kind, I am in full possession of the law and have the power to make such a decision. It is set forth in the original writings of the Law of Houses which are sealed in the house of Carcescu, that were drafted by the Original one himself. I am not at fault for your lack of knowledge or the fact that you did not bother to know where you stood before you began your campaign. Hence, my decision remains unaltered."

"You are correct about one thing, Pathos, the original charter does say that there must be four houses. Therefore, this night, I will bring a new house into the fold. They will be known as the house of 'Nataar' which means the Guardians, and the newest inhabitants will be the four who attempted to stand against your tyranny. The remaining line of the house of Dvorak may either join this house or take refuge in any of the other three. In any case, no one will remember the name of Pathos after this night except in stories told as a cautionary tale against treachery."

"You will be the one facing the Keeper when the Original one awakes! He will avenge the wrong being done to me this night, you Algaerian dog!" Pathos screamed.

Pathos was so overcome by rage that he was not in his right mind. Without taking time to consider his actions, he attempted to rush Dmitri, sword in hand; who quickly stepped aside and with his own sword, took Pathos' right arm cleanly at his elbow, watching it fall to the ground with a dull thud. The severed hand still clutched the sword it held. With a subsequent slashing motion, Dmitri cut into Pathos' midsection and watched the blood begin to spill slowly. The blood flow was not fast enough to kill him with his healing power, just fast enough to momentarily slow him down. All were silent and in awe of what they had just witnessed. Dmitri then raised his hand in a beckoning motion. Three cloaked figures in black hooded robes came forward. As the leader of the group pulled back the hood of his cloak, there was an audible intake of breath from Aconia. Ruslan!

As the Keeper stepped forward to acknowledge his duty, he looked momentarily at Aconia and met her gaze. She had not known what had become of him all those centuries ago when he had set her free and urged her to run. She only knew that he must have made it to Dmitri because she had been freed from Pathos' grasp, but she had never really heard what had become of him. Now she knew. He was a Keeper.

Aconia rushed toward him, "How, how is this possible?" she asked him directly unable to hide her shock and surprise as she looked him over from top to bottom to make sure it was really him who was standing before her.

"When I told you to run all those years ago, I ran too. I made it to Dmitri as was the plan, but because I had disobeyed my master and had born witness against him, which was still to be proven, it might have been me who ended up in the hands of the Keeper. However, the last Keeper had faithfully served his time and was ready to retire to a lasting sleep until the end of time. One was needed to replace him. I took his place in exchange for a pardon. Forgive me Aconia, I only wanted to save you from the slavery I had already known for several centuries." She hugged him fiercely, not wanting to let him go but knowing she must. She whispered in his ear to live for many centuries and never look back. He whispered back that she must do the same. Then, with a bittersweet smile that showed more in her eyes than on her face, she stepped back to make way for the proceedings to continue.

As Pathos was brought forward to face justice, he began to laugh maniacally. "You would deliver me into the hands of the Keeper, but you are the true ill of our race Dmitri. You force our kind to live in shadows like peasants and milkmaids almost in fear of the human ilk."

"It is true, I do force our kind to live in shadows, so that we may live and prosper for many millennia, not just for the present day. Unless you've forgotten Pathos, it was your house and sire line; the house of Dvorak, which nearly brought us to the brink of extinction not one hundred years ago.

"Because of your careless and reckless pursuits. I have spent the last seventy years restoring order. It appears that I will have to do the same here as well, but hopefully not for as long." With that, Pathos was led away into the distance. The group stopped about two hundred yards away. The two guards who flanked Pathos forced him to kneel upon the earth as they began to hum in a chant, which gradually became a song. Ruslan began to chant with them. It was the song of death which ushers a new arrival into the next realm. As the others looked on, they could see the glint on the blade of Ruslan's sword as he raised it high into the air, and then with sudden swift fury brought it down; taking Pathos' head from his body. Pathos' head hit the ground like a ripened coconut. All were silent and the three keepers slowly turned and walked away, gradually disappearing into the night as Pathos' body began to desiccate, being carried away as dust on the wind.

Dmitri looked at Jeremy and bade him come forth. Jeremy did as he was asked.

"I commend your bravery, although I know that this was not your choice, to be part of this world." he said. "You are welcome to stay with us if you wish and your friends the same, although to be fair, I believe that they have already chosen to remain. "You were not allowed a choice in this matter, and while I am not able to remove the curse upon you now because you have already fed, I can hold it at bay for a time, to give you a time of choosing that I was never given. With that, Dmitri took one of the chains he wore about his neck and placed it around Jeremy's neck. This will keep the promise that I have made you. Jeremy regarded the deep violet jewel hanging from the chain with awe. You will have several years in which to live your nearly human life and to decide which world you will ultimately belong to. Your senses will be muted. This means you will still possess slightly heightened senses and abilities, a bit above that of an average human, but not as much as a vampire. This is because your transition is not quite fully complete. You will be able to walk about in daylight for half a day, but you will begin to become ill if you are in daylight for too long a time. You will continue to age as the living do, but at a much slower pace. At the end of this time period, we will come to you and at that time you must choose. If you choose to remain in the human world, you will forfeit your life, as the curse cannot be undone. If you choose to live in our world, you will join our legions and become one of us. You will have the choice of joining the house of Algaerius or remaining with the house of Nataar should you so choose, and bring with you, whomever you choose as your second. This I decree before you this night."

Jeremy stood stock still for a second, attempting to mentally process all that he had seen, heard, and been a part of that evening. He looked at Dmitri, who it was still difficult to look at directly because of the sheer power and strength he exuded.

"I would like to remain in the human world for a time. I need time to break away." Jeremy said.

"I understand," Dmitri responded. "I also did not choose this life, but it was given to me when I was critically wounded during a fierce conflict. It took me more than a century to reconcile my existence in this life. Remember you can tell no one of the human world the truth of your existence, or ours. It is forbidden, and to do so you would forfeit all that you have already gained this night. This goes for your friend as well." Dmitri said as he looked toward Mike who held up a hand in a scout's honor type of gesture to affirm his understanding.

"I understand," Jeremy responded quietly, and with that it was done. Dmitri and Sjoren said their goodbyes to the group and took to the sky as twilight was beginning to break over the horizon. The large moon was still visible but was also beginning to fade. The others hastily bid Jeremy goodbye and crept away to darkened shelters to sleep away the day.

As Jeremy stood there and watched daylight break over the horizon for the first time in months, he felt an exhilaration he had not known since before becoming a vampire. Mike came toward him, a smile creeping across his face.

"You made it; you survived the night," Mike said, clapping him on the back of the shoulder.

"Yes, and I have been allowed a time of choosing as well. At the end of that time, I will be required to declare my allegiance, but for now I am free. Free to live as I want."

"Well then, I guess we had better let your parents know you are safe. After that, I think I might head down the road a bit. I think this town has given me enough adventure lately to last a lifetime."

"Yes, I know what you mean," Jeremy replied. With that, the two who were now friends began walking toward town. As Jeremy walked, he silently wondered what the coming years would bring—both for him and for the others....

About Atmosphere Press

Atmosphere Press is an independent, full-service publisher for excellent books in all genres and for all audiences. Learn more about what we do at atmospherepress.com.

We encourage you to check out some of Atmosphere's latest releases, which are available at Amazon.com and via order from your local bookstore:

Dancing with David, a novel by Siegfried Johnson

The Friendship Quilts, a novel by June Calender

My Significant Nobody, a novel by Stevie D. Parker

Nine Days, a novel by Judy Lannon

Shining New Testament: The Cloning of Jay Christ, a novel by Cliff Williamson

Shadows of Robyst, a novel by K. E. Maroudas

Home Within a Landscape, a novel by Alexey L. Kovalev

Motherhood, a novel by Siamak Vakili

Death, The Pharmacist, a novel by D. Ike Horst

Mystery of the Lost Years, a novel by Bobby J. Bixler

Bone Deep Bonds, a novel by B. G. Arnold

Terriers in the Jungle, a novel by Georja Umano

Into the Emerald Dream, a novel by Autumn Allen

His Name Was Ellis, a novel by Joseph Libonati

The Cup, a novel by D. P. Hardwick

The Empathy Academy, a novel by Dustin Grinnell

Tholocco's Wake, a novel by W. W. VanOverbeke

Dying to Live, a novel by Barbara Macpherson Reyelts

Looking for Lawson, a novel by Mark Kirby

Yosef's Path: Lessons from my Father, a novel by Jane Leclere Doyle

ABOUT THE AUTHOR

D.R. Selkirk lives in a small Northern California city with family and friends who provide countless inspirations for the stories she writes.

This is the first story about Jeremy and the friends he makes, as he struggles to make his way from one world to another. In the second story, *The Blood of Innocence*, Jeremy's adventure continues.

.